The dog laid his head and one large paw on Monte's knee. "I'm a coward, Ralph."

He gently pulled the dog's soft ears, letting them slide through his fingers. "You've got a yellow-bellied marmot for a master." Ralph's tail whacked the footstool on one side and thumped the table leg on the other.

"No more."

Ralph pricked his ears at the harsh tone of his master's voice.

"No more cowardice. I've let fear rob me of love and family. I'm forty years old and going gray, Ralph. I don't want to live out my days alone. There's a woman who might consider marrying me if I'm ever brave enough to ask. If she's the woman I think she is. . ." Sudden doubt made him falter. "I'd better make sure before I stick my neck out too far."

Even if Marva Obermeier did turn out to be his newspaper sweetheart, what if she turned up her nose at the thought of. . . of his past? Had she been able to overhear his confession from her position on the cabin porch? Her manner had been reserved rather than friendly.

He had better advance cautiously.

JILL STENGL is an award-winning author. She lives in the Northwoods of Wisconsin in a log house on a lake, along with her husband, Dean, and their two younger children, Jim and Peter. Their oldest, Tom, is an officer in the U.S. Air Force, and their daughter, Anne Elisabeth, is a junior in college. Along with her writing, Jill continues to homeschool Peter and serves as housemaid to three spoiled kitties. Jill enjoys writing fiction that portrays God's involvement in the lives of everyday people throughout history. Jill's Web page is www.jillstengl.com.

Books by Jill Stengl

HEARTSONG PRESENTS

HP197—Eagle Pilot
HP222—Finally, Love
HP292—A Child of Promise
HP335—Time for a Miracle
HP387—Grant Me Mercy
HP431—Myles from Anywhere
HP611—Faithful Traitor

Lonely in Longtree

Jill Stengl

Heartsong Presents

A note from the Author:
I love to hear from my readers! You may correspond with me by writing:

Jill Stengl
Author Relations
PO Box 721
Uhrichsville, OH 44683

ISBN 978-1-59789-385-5

LONELY IN LONGTREE

All scripture quotations are taken from the King James Version of the Bible.

All of the characters and events in this book are fictitious. Any resemblance to actual persons, living or dead, or to actual events is purely coincidental.

Our mission is to publish and distribute inspirational products offering exceptional value and biblical encouragement to the masses.

PRINTED IN THE U.S.A.

prologue

March 1891, Minocqua, Wisconsin

"Need anything else, Mr. Van Huysen?"

"Just my mail, ma'am."

"You got a newspaper and some big envelopes," Mrs. Daniels observed as she handed his mail over the counter. "You should come into town more often. This community hops with activity even during winter. Dances, concerts, masquerades—you ought to get more involved."

He smiled at the widow. "I keep busy. I'm too old for masquerades and such anyhow."

"Nonsense. You need to find yourself a wife. No sense in a man staying lonely in his old age."

"Hope I haven't yet reached that stage." Was she fishing for a second husband herself? Monte paid cash for his groceries, picked up two heavy sacks, and made the first trip out to his waiting sledge. He covered the sacks with oiled tarps to keep them dry. Two more trips, and he brushed off his gloves.

Sunlight tried to break through the heavy overcast. Icicles like jagged teeth glittered on the eaves of the shop and of every building along Front Street. The snow near the train station and tracks was grimy with soot, and traffic had fouled the roads. So much for a pristine wilderness.

"Wake up, Buzzard Bait." He rubbed one horse's furry ears, then gripped the other by its soft chin. Giving a little shake, he lifted until its fluttering nostrils blew steamy-warm breath into his face. "No more nap, Petunia-gal." He kissed the whiskery pink nose and straightened Petunia's tangled forelock. Both horses tried to rub their faces on his sleeves or his backside while he removed their blankets and checked their harness and hooves. "Watch it there, Buzz," he warned when the horse nearly knocked him sprawling.

The door of the general store squeaked open, and Mrs. Daniels stepped outside. "You dropped your newspaper, Mr. Van Huysen."

"Always dropping something." Monte tucked the paper under his arm. "Thank you kindly, ma'am."

"The roads are bad. You take care." The store mistress retreated into her small but warm building.

"Will do. I go mostly across the lakes anyway." But Mrs. Daniels had already closed the door. Monte climbed to the seat of his wagon set on runners, clucked to the team, and started off west along Front Street, passing a line of hotels and shops and circling the island's shoreline until he reached the landing. Other sleds and sledges had packed a smooth track down to the lake. The snow on top of the ice was light; his horses made easy work of it. Speeding across the level white plain, Monte found it hard to recapture a vision of blue summer lakes and lush green shoreline. Frigid wind burned the exposed skin around his eyes and found every niche in his outerwear armor. Weaving around islands, cutting across necks of land, he made his way back to his remote section.

Pride swelled his chest when he first glimpsed the tree-lined shore. No finer piece of land existed in the Northwoods, he firmly believed. Magnificent white pines towered above naked oaks, elms, maples, and aspens. Birch boles traced silvery streaks against the deep green of fir and spruce. At his approach, a group of deer startled into the trees, white tails bobbing and flashing.

Come spring, he would begin breaking ground for a lodge. A hunting and fishing lodge to attract the wealthy socialites of Chicago and Milwaukee. Unlike local logging towns, Minocqua staked its future on its natural beauty. Monte's dream lodge should help bring that bright future and prosperity to the Lakeland area.

He drove the team up a shore landing and along the lane he had labored to carve from his wilderness home. The horses stopped in front of his cabin and waited for him to unload. A mule brayed a noisy greeting from the paddock; Buzz whinnied in answer. Petunia only snorted. Inside the cabin, a dog bayed and scratched at the door.

"At least I don't come home to a quiet, empty house," Monte mused.

He made himself wait until evening before he opened the newspaper and put up his feet. Ralph the hound stretched on the hearth before a blazing fire. Monte lowered one foot from his stool to rub along the dog's side.

He snapped open the paper, tilted it to catch the oil lamp's beam, and started reading at the top of the front page. No article escaped his interest. Each week he found pleasure in reading accounts of mostly unknown people in a far-off town. Mr. and Mrs. Boswell Martin celebrated their ninth anniversary by traveling to Chicago to see an opera. Ole Sutton was robbed on the road just east of town; a drifter was arrested in connection with the incident. Mr. Gustaf Obermeier celebrated his sixtieth birthday with his wife, Elsa, and daughter, Marva.

A familiar name caught his eye, and he straightened in his chair. *Last week, Longtree's own Mr. Myles Van Huysen performed a benefit concert for Longtree Community Church, donating all proceeds toward a new and larger facility. The concert was a great financial success. . . .* Monte skipped over details about the proposed construction. *Mr. Van Huysen lives near town with his wife, Beulah, his children, and his paternal grandmother, Mrs. Virginia Van Huysen of Long Island, New York.*

Monte read the article three times, then stared across the room. Myles, still singing, but not for his own profit. He might have been rich and famous by now. How did his grandmother feel about her prodigy grandson's choosing a farm over a brilliant career on stage? How would Gran feel about her miscreant older grandson's new life as proprietor and owner of a recreation lodge?

A wave of loneliness for family swept over him. He closed his eyes and rubbed their lids. How old would Gran be now? She had seemed ancient twenty years ago. Had it really been twenty years? Pretty near.

What if. . . ? He pursed his lips and stared into the fire. What if he were to advertise his new lodge in the *Longtree Enquirer*? What if Myles could be tempted to bring his family north for a vacation on the lakes? Myles had always enjoyed outdoor sports. Perhaps if Monte played up the family fun aspect of the lodge. . . Maybe he could run a family special. . . . He must get a piano. . . .

The idea had merit, yet the probability of luring Myles and his family to Minocqua was laughably remote. Only God could pull off such a miracle. And Monte didn't dare ask Him, since God would ask in return, reasonably enough, why he didn't simply take a train down to Longtree to mend fences with his estranged family. Why should the Lord perform a miracle to accomplish reconciliation when he could easily initiate it himself?

Moping, he skimmed through the personal ads: *16h. molly mule for sale. . .housemaid needed. . .farm auction.* Then one ad caught his full attention:

Single woman of good reputation, in possession of small but prosperous farm, requires godly man of solid character as husband. Must tolerate presence of elderly parents. I can manage a farm alone but would prefer companionship. I am healthy, average in appearance and education, and easygoing by nature. I neither expect nor desire romantic overtures. Interested parties may contact the Longtree Enquirer *for further information. Lonely in Longtree*

❧

April, Longtree, Wisconsin

Marva dumped tepid dishwater over the edge of the porch, then hurried back inside, already shivering with cold. "I think the temperature's dropping again," she commented. "The days may be getting longer, but they aren't much warmer. I'll put a hot water bottle in your bed tonight."

"No need, dear. Your father has warm feet." From her rocking chair pulled up close to the stove, Marva's mother smiled and nodded. Her knitting needles never missed a click.

Papa snorted and shook his newspaper until it crackled. "What stuff and nonsense they print in this paper!" He scooted his slippers closer to the stove, dropped the outspread paper into his lap, and tapped it with his magnifying lens. His white beard trembled in indignation. "Some fool man wrote an answer to some fool woman's advertisement for a husband. Can you imagine anything more idiotic? The man could be anything—a drunkard, a murderer, anything!"

"Or the woman could be out to trap him for his money," Mother said.

Marva set the dishpan upside-down on the drain board and wiped down the countertops, watching her damp pink hands with deep concentration.

"Our Marva would never need to advertise," Mother said dreamily. "Some man will come along and snatch her up one of these days."

Marva paused and stared through the kitchen window at the landscape of early spring. A bleak view: gray, cold, and muddy. Much like her own future.

At one time she had believed her mother's romantic predictions. At one time she had considered herself a prize. But then man after man had come into her life, and man after man had passed on to some other woman or some other town. Marva might have married a filthy deputy with a bullet head and barrel chest, but he had turned out to be crooked as well as repulsive. She might have given the nod to a certain buck-toothed, goggle-eyed farmhand by the name of Camarillo Nugget had she so chosen.

She hadn't been that desperate.

Not back then.

Back then she had trusted that God would fulfill the desires of her heart. Back then she had depended on Him to provide her with a husband.

The one worthy man she'd thought might ask to share her future had chosen a pretty young girl of nineteen instead. Not that she begrudged Myles and Beulah Van Huysen their happiness together, but no one could deny that Beulah's gain had been Marva's loss.

All these years she'd spent alone, watching other women

bear children and raise them. God must have forgotten about Marva Obermeier. That was the best she could figure.

"Time for us to turn in, Mrs. Obermeier." Papa folded up the paper, rose and stretched with a crackle of joints, and thumped his broad chest with one fist. "I'm fishing in the morning. Ice is off the ponds now."

"Yes, dear." Mother immediately wound up her yarn and stashed her work into the little wooden bin at her elbow. "Fishing, fishing. Always fishing." But her voice held no rancor. Rising to her diminutive full height, she trotted over to kiss Marva good night and passed on through to the bedroom. Papa gave Marva a whiskery kiss on the cheek and a tender smile and then followed Mother.

Marva waited for the door to clank shut and listened to their voices rise and fall in nightly conversation. Lifting her hand to her cheek where their kisses lingered, she smiled faintly.

Before their light turned out, she picked up the discarded newspaper and spread it on the kitchen table. Bringing the lamp close, she turned it up so that its golden light pooled on the pages. At the bottom of page 4, she found the response:

> *Lonely in Longtree: In answer to your advertisement posted in a March edition of the* Longtree Enquirer, *I proffer myself as a candidate for the position. Age 38 this month, never married, of sound health and character, I am a God-fearing man. I lay claim to considerable wooded property in the north of the state and plan to build come spring. Your parents are welcome. Sell the farm and stock and travel north to God's country. Or come first and see if the climate and conditions suit. If you dislike pine trees and sparkling lakes, you'll hate it here. Lucky in Lakeland.*

❧

June, Minocqua

Monte walked out of the Bank of Minocqua with a spring in his step. He would have sung or shouted had anyone questioned his broad grin. But passersby paid him no attention, and the horses tethered at the hitching rail dozed in complete indifference. He considered a visit to the barbershop or blacksmith but settled on Daniels' General Store instead.

Passing the Minocqua House Inn, he tipped his hat to a passing woman who gave him a rather unfriendly stare. Perhaps he had better moderate his expression to pleasant rather than beaming. As he entered the store, Mrs. Daniels greeted him in her cheery way and immediately announced that he had a stack of mail waiting. "Two of them newspapers. Now that we've got *The Times* here in town, maybe you could cancel that other subscription."

"I could." He accepted his mail, rolled it into a neat bundle, and tucked it under his arm.

"I hear you placed a large order from Glendenning. Pine and cedar and oak, they say, and huge beams of it. You planning to build soon?"

"As soon as possible, ma'am. A crew will begin digging the basement tomorrow. I plan to have my resort up and running by next summer." He met her curious gaze with a pleasant smile.

"You know they've got the ferry running to the Hazelhurst road now, and a drug store is going in across the way. This town is booming! I wish you luck with your resort, Mr. Van Huysen. What are you planning to call it?"

"I haven't yet decided."

"Did you have a nice visit to Wausau? Word is that you

visited the land office and bought up your claim. Wherever did you get the money for that? Rumors are flying all over town!"

"I had a pleasant visit to Wausau, Mrs. Daniels, although the train north ran twenty minutes late. Ma'am, I'm thinking I don't need to subscribe to *The Times*. I've got you to keep me informed of all the local news."

She stared for a moment, then chuckled. "Mr. Van Huysen, you're such a card! Now you take care."

He paused in the doorway to tip his hat. "And you, ma'am."

Petunia waited for him at Doyle's Livery. As soon as he entered and spoke to the proprietor, he heard his mare's welcoming whinny. "It do beat all the way that animal fancies you," Michael Doyle said after sending his stable boy to bring the horse out and saddle her up.

Monte paid for his horse's overnight keep, then sat on an outside bench to wait. Summer traffic rattled past on Chippewa Street. He found it difficult to recall how the island had appeared just a few short years ago—a peaceful cathedral of towering pines, their lofty tops whispering secrets on every breeze. If only more of those trees had been spared to shade and beautify the new town. . .

Homesteaders and developers seemed intent on stripping their land of trees. He could not understand this compulsion. Why should progress always destroy beauty? Tourists flocked to Minocqua for its natural attractions. His lodge, he determined anew, would complement its surroundings and satisfy a tourist's hunger for nature unspoiled.

Recalling his two newspapers, he unrolled one and scanned its pages for a note from Lonely in Longtree. If another month passed without a response, he would give up. Responding to that ad had been a foolish whim anyway.

No reply in the older paper. Trying to ignore a sense of disappointment, he opened the second one. *To Lucky in Lakeland*—his breath caught.

Clop, clop, clop. "Here she is, Mr. Van Huysen."

Petunia butted her head into the open newspaper and nearly tossed it to the ground. Monte's flash of anger expired as soon as he glimpsed the mare's affectionate expression. "Rotten beast that you are," he said, hugging her head as she lipped his shirt buttons.

"I like your horse, Mr. Van Huysen."

"So do I, son." He slipped the lad two coins and a wink.

"Thanks!"

With his mail safely stowed in the saddlebags, he headed north on the Minocqua and Woodruff Road, letting Petunia choose her pace. "Thanks to your interruption, I didn't have a chance to read her response. I sure hope this isn't a goodbye letter or a 'no, thank you.' I reckon you think I'm crazy, girl, but this little correspondence is the most fun I've had in years. Well. . .woman type of fun, anyway. I'll admit I've had some fun reeling in a walleye upon occasion." He grinned and patted the mare's sleek neck.

Much of the enjoyment lay in anticipation. Playing games with himself, he put off reading the ad. Only after his stock had been fed and after a leisurely stroll with his hound along the lakeshore, listening to the warning warble of loons and the incongruously twittering call of a soaring bald eagle, did he allow himself the pleasure of satisfied curiosity. Settling into a chair on the shore, he snapped open the newspaper and read:

To Lucky in Lakeland: Your offer intrigues, yet I find your suggestions improper at this point in our acquaintance. I would know more about a man than his age and property before I would travel anywhere to meet him. Please describe your situation in greater detail if indeed your offer is serious. Why should I leave my home and move north when I already possess a comfortable situation here? The name "Lucky" carries unattractive connotations. Do you gamble? Smoke? Drink? I require a man of virtue whose life reflects genuine fear of God, not lip service. Lonely in Longtree.

Monte gazed blindly across the lake. . .and smiled.

one

Delight thyself also in the LORD*;*
and he shall give thee the desires of thine heart.
PSALM 37:4

Summer 1893

A blessed hush dropped over the train coach. Doubtful that the peace could last, Marva glanced from side to side, gently bobbing eight-month-old Ginny on her shoulder. To her right, Jerry, age eight, slumped against her arm. To her left, Joey, age four, dozed in his seat, still clutching a toy horse in each hand.

Marva heaved a restrained sigh. Ginny stirred, and Marva resumed patting the baby's backside. Motherhood was exhausting. . .and these weren't even her children. How did Beulah manage at home? Probably the children weren't as restive in familiar surroundings. The constant motion and clamor of the train, the cinder-thick air, the heat, and the press of humanity must be nearly unbearable to a child. It was bad enough for an adult who understood why such discomfort must be endured.

Not that Marva was certain of the reasons herself. This "vacation" had been anything but restful thus far. She felt like an unpaid nanny. . .although, to be fair, she had offered her help repeatedly. How could any decent person watch friends struggle to control and comfort their six restless and bored children and *not* offer to help?

She should have stayed home to care for the farm. Traveling in company with all married adults and children served only to emphasize her singleness. She should have seen her parents off at the train station with a wave and a blessing. Ridiculous to imagine that—

The front coach door opened, and Myles Van Huysen entered. He met Marva's gaze and smiled, making his way along the narrow aisle. After a quick glance at his sleeping offspring, he shook his head with a rueful smile. "How'd you do it? You're amazing, Marva," he said in hushed tones. "Want me to take over? Beulah finally got Trixie to sleep. Tim and Cy are with the Schoengard family."

The children might wake when she moved, but their father would simply have to handle that eventuality. Marva's every joint ached from hours of immobility. She handed Ginny to Myles, who cradled his baby girl expertly. Extricating herself from between the two boys was more difficult, but Marva managed it with only a few minor mishaps—such as pulling the hair of the man seated in front of her when she grasped the top of his seat for leverage and crushing her hat when she reached up into the luggage rack overhead. Once in the aisle, she straightened her back and legs, expecting to hear the crackle and pop of petrified joints. But the train whistled at that propitious moment, so any evidence of fossilization was concealed.

Myles took her place between his boys. Jerry wrapped his hands around his father's arm and snuggled down to sleep again. Joey slumped across Myles's lap.

Feeling a sudden need for air, even the smoky air on the platform, Marva staggered to the back of the lurching coach and outside, where she clutched the railing and breathed deeply. As long as she didn't look down, the speed wasn't too dizzying. To her delight, trees obscured her view. When had the scenery switched from farmland to forest? Absorbed in entertaining the children and calming the baby, she hadn't so much as glanced out the train's windows in several hours.

The clacking of the rails changed in tone as the train crossed a bridge over a blue river, and then the train flashed back into the cool stillness of forest on the far side.

A gust of smoke swept over her. Coughing, she blinked cinders from her eyes and made a futile attempt to wave away the choking fumes. Her white shirtwaist was now gray with black speckles. Enough of enjoying the scenery. She hurried back inside.

Near the back of the coach, her parents sat peacefully reading and dozing. Mother smiled at Marva's approach. "No children?"

Marva pulled her small valise from the overhead rack. "Myles took them. I think I'll try to catch a few winks."

"Your father says we should arrive within the hour. Isn't the view splendid? I'm so thankful you came with us, dearest. I know you've always wanted to travel and see the world."

She'd been thinking more along the lines of New York, Boston, or even Paris, but the Northwoods would have to suffice for the present. Marva returned her mother's smile. "The trees are magnificent. What are you reading, Papa?"

He closed the book over his finger and gave her a sheepish grin. "It's a Western novel I borrowed from Timmy Van Huysen."

"Once a boy, always a boy." Mother patted his arm.

The book jacket portrayed a cowboy astride a rearing horse on a narrow ledge above a cliff. His rifle spouted lurid orange flame at an attacking mountain lion. Instead of remarking on the hero's obviously imminent demise or the lion's improbably scarlet mouth, Marva said only, "My, but he wears furry trousers."

"Those are chaps," Papa grumbled and returned to reading. "Women!"

"I'm thankful this is a fishing trip and not a lion-hunting expedition. I'm picturing you in furry chaps straddling a wild mustang." Marva smiled at the thought.

"Those days are long past for me." He glanced up at her again. "You used to enjoy fishing."

"Oh, perhaps I'll try it again if you wish, but this trip promises to be more of a babysitting ordeal for me than anything adventurous."

Although she had tried to keep her tone light, her mother's eyes narrowed. "Marva, you are under no obligation to watch anyone's children."

She tried to forestall a lecture. "I can hardly enjoy myself if I know Beulah is exhausted and miserable. I was merely funning. I'm sure I'll find time to catch a bluegill or two." She glanced around in search of empty seats. "If I'm asleep when we arrive, please don't leave me on the train."

"Wouldn't matter much if we did," her father said, "since Minocqua is the end of the line."

Three rows up, she plopped into a window seat and set her bag beside her. Across the aisle sat a pair of strangers, sleeping soundly from all appearances.

Marva opened her valise and dug around until she located an envelope. Holding it to her chest, she glanced around once more. No one was looking. She pulled out a few newspaper clippings.

Lucky in Lakeland. For two years they had maintained an awkward association by newspaper ads. Sometimes months had passed between notes, yet each time she had thought the correspondence might be finished, another note would appear in the paper. For two years she had waited for him to make some kind of move, some indication that he wanted their relationship to advance.

He often spoke of her and her parents coming north, but no definite invitation had been extended, no names had been exchanged. The entire situation was distressingly indefinite.

She squeezed her eyes shut.

Most likely, Lucky, as she now thought of him, had simply entertained himself for two years by encouraging a desperate spinster. Still, he sounded sincere. . . .

Lonely in Longtree: I am not a gambling man, and neither do I smoke or drink—although I indulged in all these vices in my distant past. God changed my life. I actually consider myself blessed but chose "lucky" for the alliteration. You are right to demand more information. In December of last year, I filed claim on a section within easy distance of several local towns, located on the shore of a sizable fishing lake, rich in wildlife and quality lumber, and, in short, representing my idea of heaven on earth. Having made substantial improvements to date, I recently purchased the acreage and intend to begin construction of a resort lodge. Might you take interest in such a venture? Lucky and Blessed in Lakeland.

She ran her finger over the yellowed slip of paper. The man might have deceived her these past two years. He might prove a fraud. But she still felt vindicated in writing to him on the basis of those four powerful words: "God changed my life."

Dear Lonely in Longtree, I intend to hire a cook, a housekeeping staff, etc. Your role here would be entirely your choice. I hoped you might enjoy the venture as much as I do. Construction has started, and the log walls are going up. I wish you could come and see. Plenty of room for your parents to either live in the lodge or have a comfortable cabin of their own. Do you enjoy reading? Lucky in Lakeland.

Back then he had sounded eager to meet her, to show her his lodge. But somehow their discussions had rambled away from relationship into surface matters. Discussions of reading preferences and leisure pastimes had their merits, yet the friendship had never deepened. Did Lucky possess depths of character? Or perhaps he was the type of man who would always keep a woman shut out of his inner life.

But what did she expect? Any woman silly enough to bypass convention and advertise for a husband in the newspaper shouldn't expect a perfect match. Any woman sinful enough to bypass God's leading and strike out on her own couldn't expect rich blessings.

She slid the clippings back into the envelope, careful to keep them neat and orderly. His notes had revealed many clues to his identity. She knew that the train brought his mail into town, so he lived near a railroad line. She knew the approximate date his town had been founded. He owned and operated a new resort built from logs and located on a lake. He was unmarried, which she could only hope proved true, forty years old, clean living, and exceptionally well educated.

A lifetime habit of prayer prompted her to whisper, "Dear God, I know I shouldn't have started this mess in the first place, but please help me to find him."

Yet even as she spoke the words, a conflict rose within her.

In the vast Northwoods of Wisconsin, locating one man who did not wish to be located would be nothing short of miraculous. Why should she expect God to bless her rebellion? If He had provided her with a suitable husband in the first place, she wouldn't have been tempted to advertise for a man. But then again, God knew she would advertise before she ever picked up the pen to write that first inquiry, so why shouldn't He bless her feeble efforts to force His hand?

❧

Monte strolled along the train platform, his gaze scanning the sky until he found a circling pair of eagles—two dots against the blue. A gentle breeze rippled the lake, scattering the reflected trees. A horse's snort gave him an inward start, and he realized how tense he had become. This would never do.

He swung his arms back and forth and rolled his head from side to side until his neck crackled. He sucked in a deep breath and exhaled noisily, attempting a grin.

It was no good. Nothing could lure his thoughts away from the approaching confrontation. For weeks, doubts and speculations had milled within the enclosure of his mind like corralled mustangs, determined to break free. No matter how diligently he reinforced the fences with known facts, those wild-eyed doubts kicked and pushed and jostled until the facts splintered and fell. Wriggling through the gaps, the ugly worries stampeded his composure.

He wanted a drink. More than once he cast a glance along Front Street toward St. Elmo's Saloon. It had been years. Many long years. Surely one drink to bolster his nerves wouldn't offend the Almighty.

To distract himself, he returned to check the lineup of Lakeland Lodge wagons waiting near the depot amid vehicles from other hotels and lodges. Petunia and Buzz nickered at the sight of him, and he placed his hands on their faces for comfort. His own comfort.

Forty-two guests would soon arrive. Not his first large party; he'd had several. His drivers would competently convey the tourists and their luggage to Lakeland Lodge, where uniformed staff would direct them to their rooms or cabins. His cook and kitchen crew were even now preparing a divine repast for the evening meal. A small fleet of boats awaited the arrival of eager fishermen.

He felt confident of his lodge and its staff. They could not fail to please. No doubts on that score rankled his mind.

"Monte," one of the drivers, who was also his friend and business partner, called out. "I see smoke away down the line. Train's coming."

He waved acknowledgment. "Thanks, Hardy."

Selling a half interest in the business had allowed Monte more free time to continue his writing. Harding "Hardy" Stowell was a good businessman and a brother in the Lord.

His worries whipped back like a compass needle returning to NORTH. How long had it been since he last saw Myles? Eighteen years? Nineteen? What if he didn't recognize his own brother? What if, when he revealed his identity, Myles hopped back on the train and took his family with him? What if. . . ? What if. . . ?

Rising panic finally drove him to pray. "Lord," he muttered through his teeth, "help me face him. Give me strength to admit how weak I've been." Imagining a look of disappointment and condemnation on his brother's face, he grimaced. "I don't have any idea what to say. I should never have done this."

A distant train whistle brought his head up. Black smoke drifted above the treetops across the lake. Monte returned to the platform. His leg bones must have liquefied. Bile rose in his throat. He swallowed hard and felt nauseous.

The locomotive's brakes started screeching while it was still on the trestle. Its deep *chuff, chuff* slowed, and the great billowing monster finally halted with its passenger cars beside the platform. Steam hissed in a white plume from its side.

He could hardly bear to watch the passengers disembark. The sun's heat became unendurable. His mouth was parched.

Laughing, talking people descended the steps, gathered on the platform, and stared at their surroundings with evident interest. Children ducked and scrambled amid the legs and skirts. One man made a grab at a young boy, catching him by the back of his jacket.

It was Myles.

two

Fear thou not; for I am with thee: be not dismayed;
for I am thy God: I will strengthen thee; yea, I will help thee;
yea, I will uphold thee with the right hand of my righteousness.
Isaiah 41:10

Monte recognized his younger brother instantly, not by his appearance—which had changed over the years—but by his graceful movements and an indefinable quality in his bearing.

"Myles," he whispered the name.

"Mr. Stowell?"

A tall, burly man with graying blond hair had approached Monte unnoticed.

"Uh, no. Mr. Stowell is over there." He nearly introduced himself, but indecision tied his tongue in a knot. Hardy had handled all reservations and business with this group from Longtree.

"But you're with Lakeland Lodge, aren't you?"

Monte nodded.

"David Schoengard here. I'm a minister." Rev. Schoengard smiled and shook Monte's hand. "It was a long ride, but we're here at last."

"Welcome to Minocqua. The town isn't much to look at, but wait until you see the lodge." To his surprise, his voice sounded normal.

Only dimly aware of his actions and praying in his heart, he supervised the loading of luggage, including fishing poles and tackle. "You people are serious about your fishing," he said to a bearded old gentleman waiting near the wagon hitched to Petunia and Buzz.

"That we are, sir." Anticipation gleamed in the man's faded blue eyes. "Are you our driver?"

"I am." Monte climbed into the wagon bed, slid a valise beneath one of the bench seats, and arranged fishing poles along a side panel. "You've never had better fishing than you'll find around here."

"This is a lifetime opportunity. I've read the advertisements for this lodge in our local newspaper these past many months and dreamed about landing one of those record muskellunge."

Monte climbed down and gripped the man's surprisingly powerful hand. "I sincerely hope your dreams will come true, Mr. . . ?"

"Obermeier. Gustaf Obermeier, sir. And this is my wife, Elsa, and our daughter. . . . Ah, well, she's here somewhere."

"She's helping Beulah with the children," Mrs. Obermeier said. "What is your name, sir?"

"Just call me Monte." He tipped his head toward the wagon. "Your luggage is loaded. I imagine you're eager to reach the lodge and start fishing."

Mrs. Obermeier chuckled. "Please don't tempt him, Mr. Monte. Morning will be soon enough for that, I should think."

He took the woman's elbow to assist her into the wagon.

"Mother!" Rapid footsteps clopped on the platform.

Mrs. Obermeier turned back. "There you are, dear. Are you riding with us or with the Van Huysens?"

Hearing that name gave Monte a jolt.

"Beulah asked me to ride with them—the children are nearly beside themselves with excitement. I'll rejoin you at the lodge."

The younger woman spoke rapidly. She had a rich-sounding voice. Monte wondered which man in the party claimed her as his wife. That ash-blond hair of hers would catch any man's attention.

As she walked away, more guests climbed into Monte's wagon: a young couple who behaved like newlyweds and a family of four whose names he missed. While Monte clucked up the horses, his passengers launched into happy discussion of the coming weeks. They mentioned names he found vaguely familiar, probably from seeing them in news articles.

At times he glimpsed Hardy's wagon ahead on the road. Myles and his family were in that wagon, he knew. Sunlight glinted off the lake alongside the Minocqua and Woodruff Road. In summer there could be no cutting across the lakes to shorten the trip home, but the local roads were in decent-enough repair. "What lake is this, Mr. Monte?" one of the women asked.

"Just Monte, ma'am; no 'mister,' please. It's called Kawaguesaga Lake. Up ahead here the road splits off, and we'll head west toward the Lac du Flambeau reservation." He jiggled Petunia's reins to wake her up.

"Will we see any Indians while we're here?"

"You're likely to, ma'am."

"Are they friendly?" Mr. Obermeier asked.

"Mostly." He shrugged. "They're like any people—some are friendly; some are not. One of the lodge's fishing guides is Ojibwa. We call him Ben. If he can't find you a big fish, no one can."

They again conversed among themselves, leaving Monte to his thoughts. When would be the best time to approach Myles? Probably not tonight, while the children were overtired and ornery. In the morning, perhaps? But he could never wait that long! Somehow he had pictured himself walking up to Myles on the station platform to reveal his identity, but that idea had fizzled. Myles and his wife had been far too preoccupied with controlling their numerous offspring even to notice his presence.

The lead wagons turned off the main road. "Are we nearly there?" asked one of the men.

"I'm sorry, but the lodge is a good distance off yet," Monte said.

"No need to apologize, Monte." Mr. Obermeier sounded tired but cheery. "We all hoped for adventure in the wilderness."

Monte smiled back over his shoulder. The old man had pluck.

When the lodge appeared between the trees, along with the glimmer of the lake beyond, a chorus of appreciative gasps and exclamations lifted Monte's spirits. "Is this the same lake that surrounds the town of Minocqua?" Mr. Obermeier asked.

"Yes and no. This lake is linked to that one by a channel. However, both parts of the lake chain are called Lake Kawaguesaga at present. It gets confusing."

"The lodge is magnificent," the little bride said in evident satisfaction. "George, I'm so glad now that we came here for our honeymoon and not Niagara Falls. You were right."

Monte left his wagon for the hired men to unload and escorted his party of guests into the large foyer. A quick glance around for Myles left him frustrated once again. He checked the register to remind himself which cabin his brother's family had reserved. Number Five. The largest. If he'd been thinking clearly, he would have guessed as much.

"After you register, head into the dining room where supper is presently being served. Your luggage will be delivered to your rooms or cabins."

The little group of guests thanked him and moved on about their business.

It might be kinder to wait until Myles and his wife had time to settle their children for the night, but this protracted delay was destroying his nerves. Taking a deep breath, he gazed around the crowded lobby. The staff worked smoothly and efficiently. He felt a moment's pride; the lodge was everything he had envisioned, thanks in large part to Hardy Stowell's business expertise.

If all went as he hoped and planned, Monte would be able to relax and enjoy this next month.

That was a mighty big *if.*

❧

"Miss Obermeier, I hope and pray your visit here at Lakeland Lodge will be some of the best days of your life."

Marva watched Mr. Harding Stowell twist his hat between his hands and took pleasure in his evident admiration. "Thank you, sir."

"If you need anything—anything at all—just send word."

"I'll do that, Mr. Stowell."

He finally clapped his hat back on his head and walked down the cabin's steps. Marva watched him for a moment, smiling to herself. He was about the right age, single, a Christian man, well educated. . .and rather endearingly socially inept. Although she couldn't be certain he was "Lucky," her suspicion had strong grounds.

She might have wished for a bit more physical appeal in a potential husband, but she supposed his looks would grow on her as she learned to love the man within. He couldn't help his plain features.

Yet it seemed too coincidental that her correspondent beau should be the first man she encountered in Minocqua, the owner of Lakeland Lodge. Not that God couldn't do miracles, but. . . Well, time would tell.

At Beulah's request, the lodge kitchen staff brought food to the Van Huysens' cabin for the exhausted children and parents. Marva helped feed the hungry brood, told stories and sang songs to Cyrus, Jerry, and Joey, and tucked the three middle boys into bed. When she finally left the darkened bunkroom, leaving the door slightly ajar, her body and head ached.

Beulah and Myles sat in matched rocking chairs near the stone fireplace. Ginny snuggled against her mother's shoulder, her eyes half-closed. Trixie clung to her father and wailed, her face pink and damp. Both parents gave Marva apologetic looks.

"What would we have done without you today?" Beulah sighed. "Are they asleep?"

"Very nearly." Marva glanced around. "Where's Tim?"

Myles tipped his chin and his gaze upward. "In the loft. He's claimed it as his hideout."

Trixie's crying increased in volume. "Stubborn little creature," her father said in evident frustration. "She's been crying for three hours now."

"I'll put Ginny down and take Beatrix for a while so you can unpack your things," Beulah said, rising slowly.

Rap, rap, rap at the cabin door.

The three adults exchanged glances. "I'll get it," Marva offered.

A man stood on the porch, lantern in hand. "Uh, is this the Van Huysens' cabin?" He removed his hat.

Marva recognized him but couldn't place his identity. "Yes, it is. How may I help you?"

"I need to talk to Myles Van Huysen." The man's eyes had

a desperate look. Uncertain, Marva glanced back at Myles for direction.

"I'll talk to him." Myles spoke over Trixie's wails and stood up.

Marva turned back. "You may come in, but please be quiet, sir. We're just now getting the children to sleep." She pushed at the screen door. He opened it and stepped inside, then stood there shuffling his hat between his hands. Marva's curiosity rose.

Myles stepped forward and extended his hand from beneath his daughter's trailing nightgown. "Good evening, sir. Is there a problem?"

The man opened his mouth, closed it, and took Myles's hand. Sweat gleamed on his forehead, though the night air was cool. "I—I—Hello, little brother."

Utterly confused, Marva stared back and forth between their rigid faces. Trixie flailed in her father's arms, but Myles seemed oblivious even when her arm struck his jaw. The color drained from his ruddy face.

"Monte?" he whispered.

Marva backed toward the kitchen area, feeling entirely out of place during this family moment. To her relief, Beulah emerged from the bedroom, studied the two men, and then approached to stand beside her husband. Trixie climbed into her mother's arms. Myles let her go, his gaze still locked with the stranger's.

Then the two men embraced, both speaking at once in choked-sounding voices.

"You were dead!"

"I'm so sorry!"

"How can this be?"

"I wanted to see you—"

Beulah looked at Marva, then back at the men, her eyes full

of questions. Trixie's cries rose in volume, as she jounced in Beulah's arms.

"I'll take her so you can talk," Marva said. "We'll go out on the porch." She took the thrashing toddler from Beulah and stepped outside.

To her surprise, Trixie fell silent and clung to her, shivering with sobs. A breeze rippled off the lake and whispered through the trees. Trixie sighed and wiped her slimy face on Marva's shoulder.

"It's so beautiful here, baby girl."

Marva heard voices rise and fall from inside the cabin. Chairs scraped on the floor and cupboard doors closed. Beulah must be preparing coffee or tea.

Little brother. Marva dredged up memories from the distant past and vaguely recalled Myles talking about a long-lost brother. How very strange that they would meet here and now! Nothing about this felt real. The entire day seemed like a misshapen dream. She shook her head, wondering if she might wake up soon.

three

Confess your faults one to another,
and pray one for another, that ye may be healed.
The effectual fervent prayer of a righteous man availeth much.
JAMES 5:16

Monte sat across the table from his brother and sister-in-law and prayed for courage. Their pale faces increased his sense of guilt. They were so tired, and now this. How could he ever make them understand? Especially when he didn't understand his own behavior or motives.

"You have a fine family." The comment sounded flat even though he meant it sincerely.

"Thank you. You've never married?" Myles, too, seemed awkward.

"No." Monte turned his coffee cup between his hands.

"Where have you been all these years? How did—?" Myles shook his head and held up both his hands in entreaty and bewilderment. "How did this happen? You here, meeting us?"

Monte pinched the bridge of his nose, still praying. "Is this a good time to tell the story? You both must be weary to death."

His brother snorted. "I'll not sleep after this. You might as well tell us."

Beulah nodded in agreement, her dark eyes wide.

"What about—? I mean, the lady outside and your little girl. . ."

"They'll be fine. Marva is almost like family," Beulah said.

He took a deep breath for fortification. "Where shall I begin?"

"I saw you get shot out of the saddle and fall into a stampede of cattle," Myles said. "All these years I thought I had watched my brother die." His voice held a hint of accusation and a world of curiosity.

Die? Monte flashed him a quick look but saw only truth in his brother's face. After taking a few deep breaths and a swig of coffee, he cleared his throat and launched into his storytelling mode of address.

"I knew Jeb Kirkpatrick was after my hide," he began. "I had owed him a bundle of money for months, and he knew I didn't have the cash. . . ."

❧

Hugging the tiny girl close, Marva hummed softly. Her back and arms ached. How long had she been out here—an hour? Every once in a while, she overheard a word or a sentence of the conversation inside the cabin. Caught between curiosity and guilt, she closed her eyes, as if that would make a difference. Sometimes the brothers raised their voices. Other times everything went so quiet that she wondered if they were all asleep.

Were they going to talk all night? Surely some of their catching up could wait for morning. She sat down on the top step, adjusted Trixie in her arms, and leaned her head against the railing. Sleep weighted her eyelids.

Some thing, or things, rustled in the shrubs near the edge of the porch.

Marva's eyes opened wide.

A shadow slipped from the shrubbery and moved along the cabin wall toward her. Glittering eyes reflected the porch lamp.

Another something burst out of the bushes and tumbled across the grass, squealing, grunting, and chattering.

Marva scrambled to her feet and rushed for the door, imagining teeth sinking into her legs at any moment.

❧

"I ended up working as a hunting guide at a Wyoming ranch that catered to rich city men with dreams of trophies hanging on their den walls. Some wanted a bear, some a bison, some an elk," Monte said. "The hardest to bring back were the bighorn sheep. Those critters are wily, nimble, and difficult to track. I befriended some members of the local Indian tribes, too."

Beulah yawned and patted her mouth. "Oh, I'm sorry!"

"I ought to let you two get some sleep." He'd been running off at the mouth like he often did when nervous.

Feet pounded on the porch, the door flew open, and the blond woman burst into the room with the tiny girl limp in her arms.

Monte and Myles both jumped to their feet.

She stopped short and returned their startled stares. "I'm sorry. I—I—Um, it was dark. . . ." She glanced down at the sleeping child. Firelight glinted on her pale hair. "Trixie is—Where do you want me to put her down?"

"There's a cot beside our bed in that room." Beulah pointed. "Marva, did something frighten you?"

"There was. . .I mean. . ." She glanced back over one shoulder. "I heard something." Her voice sounded tiny. "I saw some kind of creatures out there."

Monte quickly stepped outside to the dark porch. Moonlight sparkled on the lake's rippled surface. Small shadows waddled across the lawn area between cabins, chattering and bickering softly. *Raccoons.* A smile spread across his face as he rested his hands on the railing.

That Marva woman was really attractive. He'd heard nothing yet about a husband. . .but women that handsome didn't stay single into their thirties, which age he estimated she must be. She might be widowed. Lifting his brows, he looked back over his shoulder at the cabin door and pursed his lips in contemplation.

❧

Marva's entire face burned. "These creatures with glowing eyes came rushing at me, making strange noises. I thought of bears or. . ." She handed Trixie into Beulah's outstretched arms and covered her hot cheeks with her cold hands. "I'm sorry I interrupted. I'll leave now."

"No, you won't," Beulah said firmly. "Not until Monte can escort you to the lodge. You think we're going to let you walk back alone and be attacked by a bear? Have a cup of coffee and sit with us. You're family. You might as well hear the story." She disappeared into the cabin's bedroom.

Myles gave her a tired smile and poured a cup of coffee from the pot on the back of the stove. "It's still plenty hot."

"Are you sure?" she asked. "I mean, about my intruding on your family time."

"Yes. Why not?" He offered her sugar.

A deep voice spoke behind her. "There should be milk in the icebox." The cabin door closed.

Myles's gaze flicked past Marva. "Really? Thanks."

Reluctantly she turned to face the stranger. "I suppose there was nothing out there."

"Nothing dangerous." He smiled slowly until his white teeth showed beneath his mustache. "You'll get used to the darkness. But from now on, you'd probably best not be alone outside at night. There *are* bears in these woods, but I'll protect you."

Marva tried to smile in response to his teasing grin. This

man was too ruggedly handsome, too confident, too. . . something. She glanced back and forth between the brothers and saw the resemblance. Monte was taller and broader than Myles, with brown hair instead of red. Myles's voice held a musical quality that Monte's lacked. The likeness lay in their facial features and mannerisms.

Myles placed Marva's coffee and a jug of milk on the table. "I should introduce you. Marva, this is my brother, Montague Van Huysen. Monte, this is Miss Marva Obermeier, our long-time friend."

Marva extended her hand. Monte clasped it in a warm grasp and bowed slightly. "I am honored, Miss Obermeier. I believe I met your parents earlier."

Why was he still holding her hand? She tugged it away and tried not to let her discomposure show. "Oh. Really?"

He still gazed steadily at her face. She tried to meet his eyes but felt her throat tighten. "This is the first travel vacation they have ever taken."

That charming smile spread across his face again. "I'm glad they chose Lakeland Lodge."

Of course, his simple statement meant nothing more than the obvious.

Beulah joined them. "Thank you, Marva. She's sound asleep. I doubt cannon fire could waken her after all that crying." She turned to Monte. "I told Marva to stay until you can walk her back to the lodge."

He looked pleased. "Certainly. Are you in a hurry, Miss Obermeier?"

"No, sir."

"I haven't much more to tell, if you don't mind listening." He pulled out her chair in invitation.

"If you don't mind my hearing it, I don't mind," she said

and sat down. He scooted her chair forward, then seated himself beside her, across from Myles and Beulah.

"So go on," Myles urged.

He took a deep breath and released it slowly. "Okay, the last few years in a nutshell. One night, after a particularly exciting hunting adventure, I started writing down the day's events so I wouldn't forget. That story turned into my first published magazine article."

"You always did like to write," Myles said.

"Using my experiences, I began writing for magazines, serial stories that were later printed as books. Western novels. I write under the name 'Dutch Montana.' Somebody called me that once, and I thought it made a good pen name."

Dutch Montana? The name rang a bell inside Marva's head, but why?

Something thumped on the ceiling. The adults glanced up in time to see a pair of bare legs swing onto the loft ladder. Tim Van Huysen descended rapidly, his breathing audible in the sudden quiet.

"Tim, have you been eavesdropping?" Beulah sounded shocked.

"I couldn't help overhearing, Ma. I can't believe it! I've got a new uncle, and he's *Dutch Montana*!" The boy, still fully clothed, approached Monte boldly. His dark hair stood on end, and he clutched his pant legs at his sides.

"Howdy, Tim." Monte grinned at his nephew and shook his hand. "I'm honored that you read my books."

Tim gaped up at his uncle's face. "The fellers back home won't believe this! Would you sign my books? I brought a bundle of them."

"Sure."

"Books. That figures. No wonder your bag was so heavy,"

Myles said in amusement. "Well, sit down and join us, why don't you?"

Marva blinked as realization struck her. Papa had been reading one of Tim's Dutch Montana books on the train—that's why the name had seemed familiar to her. She felt a sudden urge to giggle over the coincidence but restrained it. No sense in advertising her overtired condition.

Monte didn't continue his tale until the boy squeezed a chair in between his parents and nestled against Myles's shoulder. "A few years back, I traveled to New York on publishing business and tried to look up the family. The prodigal returned, and all that. Problem was the fatted calf and sundry had disappeared in the meantime. I went to the old family offices and discovered that the Van Huysen Soap Company went out of business long ago, which came as a shock. After much fruitless searching, I thought of looking up Gram's old attorney. He told me to ask Mr. Poole, the detective, about you, and Poole gave me your location—in strictest confidence."

"Why all the secrecy? Why didn't you come see us then? Gram spoke of you on her deathbed." Myles's voice held an accusing note.

Monte flinched. Trying to respect his feelings, Marva kept her gaze averted and sipped her coffee. She really should have insisted on walking back to the lodge alone.

Monte took a breath and opened his mouth as if to speak but closed it again. After a long moment he tried again. "I was afraid."

"Afraid of Gram? Monte, you were the light of her eyes!"

Marva glanced over in time to see him shake his bowed head.

After a strained silence, Beulah spoke softly, "We're thankful to find you now, Monte. I imagine your grandmother is looking down from heaven and smiling to see her boys together again. She prayed faithfully for you all those years. For you and Myles both. She knew you had given your life to the Lord, Monte, and that knowledge sustained her."

He nodded. Was he crying? Marva wanted to put her hand on his arm and try to comfort him. Shocked at the very idea, she sat still and watched her own fingers trace circles on her coffee cup.

Tim rubbed at his eyes and yawned noisily.

Monte sat up straight and forged on. "I heard about land available in the Northwoods and traveled up here soon after the railroad stopped in Minocqua. I've kept track of your family from a distance these three years."

How? Marva wondered but didn't dare ask the question. She glanced up in time to see Monte cast a brotherly look at Beulah. "By the way, little brother, I must say you've found yourself a peach of a wife."

"God has blessed me, for certain."

Monte drew a deep breath, then asked, "So, Myles, what were you doing all those years after Texas? I'm pleased beyond measure to discover that God finally got through your thick skull."

"That He did, though it took years for me to pay attention. After your death—as I thought then—I drifted about, taking jobs at cattle ranches, until a great man named Obadiah "Buck" Watson hired me on to work his farm. Buck is the man whose testimony God used to change my life. Then Buck's stepdaughter stole my heart." Myles reached his arm around Tim's nodding head to touch Beulah's shoulder.

"You've made better use of your time than I have. Regrets are sorry companions, Myles. If I had been responsible all those years ago, the Van Huysen Soap Company might still be—if you'll pardon the expression—afloat, and your children would have an inheritance."

Myles shook his head. His expression seemed to blend emotional strain with spiritual peace. "Water under the bridge, Monte. You can't undo past mistakes, and blaming yourself does no one any good. The Lord had other plans for all of us. I, for one, do not regret the loss of the business, unless it was for Gram's sake. But she lived out her final years in great joy, surrounded by her great-grandchildren."

Silence fell, broken only by Tim's soft snore.

"Guess I'd better escort this young lady back to her parents," Monte said softly, scooting back his chair.

Young? Marva gave him a sharp look, suspecting the flattering remark, but he appeared unaware of having said anything questionable.

Beulah took Tim into her arms, freeing Myles to escort his brother to the door. "Good night, Monte, and welcome back to the family. Marva. . ." She paused. "Thank you."

Marva slipped around the table to give her friend a kiss on the top of her head. "You try to get some sleep, darlin'. I'm glad I could help."

Monte and Myles shook hands, then gave each other an awkward embrace. "We'll talk more tomorrow," Myles said. "Too many years to catch up on in one evening."

Monte nodded and offered Marva his arm. "Miss Obermeier?"

four

Trust in the L*ORD* *with all thine heart;*
and lean not unto thine own understanding.
PROVERBS 3:5

Moonlight scattered shadows in confusing patterns across the path as wind rustled in the trees. A loon's haunting cry floated through the night. In spite of herself, Marva shivered. Monte pressed his elbow and her hand close against his side, as if to assure her of his protection, and set a slow walking pace.

"So you're an author," she said to make conversation. That feeling of being protected was too pleasant for her emotional comfort.

"Some people think so. Others would dispute that title," he said with an undertone of amusement. "I don't claim to write great literature, by any means."

"When do you find time to write? I assume you work here at the lodge. Are you a hunting and fishing guide?"

A short pause, then he said, "I do some guiding, yes. I do most of my writing during the evenings and in winter. What do you do with your time, Miss Obermeier?"

"Mostly I help my father run the farm and help my mother run the household."

"Who's running the farm and household while you're all away?" he asked.

"My father hired a man to look after the farm, a Mr. Parker, who—*Aaack*!"

A huge, panting creature emerged from the darkness and leaped upon Monte's chest, knocking him back a step. Just as Marva drew breath for another shriek, Monte clapped his hand over her mouth, holding the back of her head with his other hand. "Hush!" he said, his voice full of laughter. "You'll have every guest in the place panicked! It's just my dog, Ralph."

She looked up at him and caught the glint of moonlight in his eyes. Humiliation rolled over her like a wave. He must think her an utter fool.

"Calm now? No more screams?"

She nodded, and he released her head. "I'm sorry I grabbed you that way. All I could think of was our sleeping guests. It's late, you know."

The dog panted and huffed around their feet, sniffed at a nearby tree, and then plunged down the slope toward the lake. "He probably caught scent of the raccoons that frightened you earlier," Monte said.

Marva's overtired brain projected images of her being clasped against this man's broad chest, his hand stroking her hair. She drew a deep breath and forged ahead on the dark trail.

He caught up with her in a few strides. "Are you all right? Miss Obermeier, I'm sorry Ralph startled you."

"I am very tired, Mr. Van Huysen."

"Call me Monte, please. Are you angry?" He seemed genuinely concerned, watching her face as he kept pace at her side. Large lanterns framing the lodge doorway guided her steps.

"I'm not angry; I'm exhausted, Mr. Van Huysen. If I awakened any of your guests, I am truly sorry. A good night's sleep should restore my good sense, but. . .how do I locate my parents' room?"

"You haven't been to your room yet?"

"No, I was helping Beulah and Myles with the children."

"We'll check at the desk." When she tripped over something on the path, he said, "Won't you please take my arm again? I know this path like I know my own face. Too many roots and rocks lying in wait to trip you up in the dark."

She laid her hand on his forearm and sensed his satisfaction. She would have to guard her heart closely against this charmer. He was nothing like serious Myles, she realized. And she liked the differences.

While Monte scanned the lodge ledger for her parents' room number, Marva studied the expansive foyer built entirely of polished logs. The antlered head of a huge deer surmounted a rock fireplace, and a standing black bear waited in the dining room doorway, its mouth open in a snarl. Thick rugs lay scattered about on the gleaming hardwood floor. Oil chandeliers made from deer antlers hung from the square-beamed ceiling, casting a romantic glow over the room. Birch boughs lined the arched doorway into what might be the dining hall. A grandfather clock located between two doors indicated ten minutes past eleven.

"The halls should be lit, but you might need a lamp once you get into your room. Wait a moment and I'll find one for you." He tapped her elbow.

She nodded. From any other man she would have resented this frequent touching, but somehow from him it seemed appropriate. She gave her head a little shake. As if rules of propriety should not apply equally to every man.

He disappeared through a door behind the desk. She suddenly felt very alone in this strange place and rubbed her arms.

"Cold?" He reappeared, a glowing lamp in hand. "I imagine

it's cooler here than in your part of the state. Wish I had a jacket to offer."

"I'll be fine, thank you." Was he this solicitous of every female guest? She could imagine women of all ages swooning over his chivalrous manners.

He offered his arm again. She looked from it to his face. "I'm sure I can find my way if you give me directions."

"Why take chances?" He opened one of the doors near the clock and indicated that she should enter first. "Quietly, please." As soon as the door closed behind him, he set the lamp on the floor, took her hand and tucked it through the crook of his elbow, and then retrieved the lamp.

Oil sconces turned low lined the hallway. "Your room is near the end on the left," he said softly.

Marva nodded and followed his lead.

Outside room 21, he stopped and turned to face her. "Take the lamp now, and keep it as long as you like. I'll see you in the morning, Miss Obermeier."

Did she imagine anticipation and warmth in his voice and eyes? He certainly had an enthusiastic personality.

"Good night, and thank you, Mr. Van Huysen." He reached behind her to open the door, and she stepped inside. After the door closed with a soft clank of the latch, she heard his footsteps fade away along the hall.

❧

As he left the lodge, Monte found himself grinning uncontrollably. What luck! No, not luck. What a blessing! Unless he was greatly mistaken, Marva Obermeier was his Lonely in Longtree. She must be! How many Christian women of her age lived alone with elderly parents and ran a farm? Well, probably hundreds did, but how many in Longtree, Wisconsin? That she and her parents should be not only acquainted but close friends with his long-lost brother defied probability. That Miss Obermeier was strikingly attractive? This fact utterly boggled his mind. Only God could arrange things so well.

Ralph approached at a gallop, panting noisily. Remembering Marva's squeals at the dog's "attack" provoked a chuckle. "Tonight you were a bear or wolf, old man," he told the dog. "Come." He slapped his leg, and Ralph heeled.

Light glowed in the window of Myles and Beulah's cabin. He looked forward to becoming acquainted with his brother's large family. Myles was a blessed man. A busy man, for certain. Six children! Monte laughed softly. If all six children proved to be as charming as young Tim, these next few weeks promised to be pleasantly entertaining.

Myles and Beulah were most likely discussing the day's surprising revelations. Remembering the friendly warmth in Beulah's eyes, Monte felt reassured. And Myles had seemed pleased, though also decidedly stunned and disturbed. How would he feel about the situation, about his brother, once he'd had time to fully consider facts? Monte knew he had plenty-more explaining to do. He felt his smile change to a frown at the worry that twisted his gut.

All this time, he had thought Myles was ashamed to acknowledge him, while in truth, Myles had thought him dead. Had he known that Myles had reconciled with God, he might have attempted a reunion sooner. But who could tell?

He entered his own cabin and flopped into his favorite chair, staring into the darkness. Ralph dropped to the floor nearby, heaving a contented sigh.

"If I had really trusted You, God, I would have approached Myles years ago," he prayed aloud.

Ralph rose and shoved his muzzle into Monte's hand.

He petted the dog absently, lost in regret. All those years he might have spent with his brother—forever lost. And never again would he see dear old Gram alive on earth.

He leaned forward in the chair, elbows on his knees, and rubbed his face with both hands. So many empty years of aimless wandering. Sure, he'd been serving God here and there, spreading the gospel message, writing his books, befriending needy people. But the longing for home and family had driven him on, never entirely at peace with himself, never satisfied.

"I suppose it could be worse, God. I could have waited until Myles and I were both doddering old codgers." He grimaced. If the church group from Longtree had not conveniently decided to vacation at his lodge, he might have waited yet another twenty years for the "right time." Shame weighted his heart.

The dog laid his head and one large paw on Monte's knee. "I'm a coward, Ralph." He gently pulled the dog's soft ears, letting them slide through his fingers. "You've got a yellow-bellied marmot for a master." Ralph's tail whacked the footstool on one side and thumped the table leg on the other.

"No more."

Ralph pricked his ears at the harsh tone of his master's voice.

"No more cowardice. I've let fear rob me of love and family. I'm forty years old and going gray, Ralph. I don't want to live out my days alone. There's a woman who might consider marrying me if I'm ever brave enough to ask. If she's the woman I think she is. . ." Sudden doubt made him falter. "I'd better make sure before I stick my neck out too far."

Even if Marva Obermeier did turn out to be his newspaper sweetheart, what if she turned up her nose at the thought of. . .of his past? Had she been able to overhear his confession from her position on the cabin porch? Her manner had been reserved rather than friendly.

He had better advance cautiously.

❧

"Push me, Miss Marba." Trixie kicked her dangling legs, red curls in chaos around her shoulders, little hands clutching the swing's ropes.

"Say please," Marva reminded.

"Pwease."

While hitching baby Ginny higher on her hip, Marva gently pushed the swing suspended from a sturdy oak branch. Trixie laughed in excitement, although she swung back and forth a total of only three feet. Watching the child's joy, Marva smiled. It took so little to please these small ones. . .yet they constantly demanded attention.

Joey played with a friend in the sandbox, content to dig and dump. The three older Van Huysen boys were off playing with friends, exploring the grounds, with strict orders from their fathers not to stray into the surrounding forest or venture into the lake. Judging by the *clank* of horseshoes and the ripples of laughter from the clearing, the other young people were finding ways to amuse themselves. The lodge seemed to be nearly filled with guests. Where had they all come from?

A breeze rustled through branches overhead—Marva was learning to love that restful sound. Blue sky and puffy clouds played backdrop to the dancing oak and maple leaves. The vivid colors nearly took Marva's breath away whenever she sneaked a glance upward. And the lake! She loved its every mood—serene, playful, agitated, intent—always in shades of blue and gray.

Myles, Beulah, and Monte were somewhere, not too far away, catching up on the past.

Again.

Still.

Twenty years was a long time, but in how much detail must it be recounted? *That Monte is a talker, for sure.* A smile twitched her lips at the thought. But then, of all people to criticize. . . She had once been notorious for being able to talk the hind legs off a donkey.

Age had brought with it an awareness of how ridiculous she'd often made herself in the sight of her friends. More than one man she had frightened away with her wagging tongue and almost frenetic energy. Not that men found her any more attractive since she withdrew into herself.

Except for Mr. Stowell, who was even now strolling down the path from the lodge. As she caught his eye, a wide smile brightened the lodge owner's face. "Miss Obermeier, how good to see you. You're looking lovely, as always."

"Good afternoon, Mr. Stowell. Finished in the office for the afternoon?"

"I wish it were so. I'm looking for Monte—Mr. Van Huysen. Have you seen him?" He paused before her. Although his words were businesslike, his eyes roved her face with an almost-rapt expression.

Was Monte in trouble with the boss for neglecting his work?

"I believe he and the other Van Huysens are down by the lake."

"Thank you. I—I hope to see you later." Mr. Stowell's face turned pink. "At supper. Perhaps you. . . Might you have time for a stroll this evening?"

"I might." It would be a good opportunity to sound him

out concerning the *Longtree Enquirer.* But then again, Beulah might need help with the children.

Mr. Stowell beamed. "Thank you." He started to say something else, stopped, and repeated, "Thank you," before moving on toward the shore.

At last, the prospect of a social moment for herself. Not that Mr. Stowell was her ideal man, but he seemed steady and pleasant, and he owned the lodge. If he did turn out to be "Lucky," he would probably make her a good, dependable husband.

A loon warbled out on the lake. Shading her eyes, Marva sought a glimpse of the bird—it sounded nearby.

Two men in a fishing boat rowed toward the shore. Her father's white beard was unmistakable. The man with him was most likely Rev. Schoengard, another devoted fisherman. She wondered if they had caught anything, but she didn't dare leave the children long enough to find out. They tied the boat to the wooden dock and hoisted their poles and tackle ashore.

Mother was probably napping in the shade with her friends. Unlike Marva, she had time to socialize with other women her age.

Self-pity crept into Marva's thoughts. After all, she had been brought along on this trip for purely practical purposes, namely as a child minder to keep the little ones from disturbing anyone else's peace. Her parents were caught up in their own activities. Marva had known this would happen when she agreed to come, but she had expected to chat with Beulah while they watched the children together.

Monte Van Huysen's presence had thrown a wrench into the clockwork, in more ways than one. Beulah told her that Monte had never married, which Marva found difficult to believe. He was far from shy, successful in his field, and appealing to the female eye. Why was he single at age forty? Probably because, Christian man though he claimed to be, he had no desire to settle down with only one woman.

She wrinkled her nose, determined to remain focused on her goal of locating and identifying Lucky in Lakeland. If only she knew a few more details about Lucky's life and his person aside from his age and his business. He seemed a serious-minded individual, articulate and responsible. Most of their conversations had centered on topics such as religion, hobbies, future plans, and dreams—topics that could freely be discussed in the open forum of a newspaper.

Lucky had claimed to enjoy fishing. She would have to ask Mr. Stowell if he pursued that hobby. Lucky had also expressed a desire to mentor young Christian men and encourage them in the faith. The memory of that particular letter started a warm glow around her heart. She could easily imagine an earnest, devout expression on Mr. Stowell's face as he expressed such a desire.

But what if she learned that Harding Stowell never read the *Longtree Enquirer*?

five

Let your conversation be without covetousness;
and be content with such things as ye have:
for he hath said, I will never leave thee, nor forsake thee.
HEBREWS 13:5

Trixie suddenly thrashed her legs in an effort to hop out of the swing. "Dog!" she cried in excitement.

A large brindle-and-white hound sniffed at a nearby tree. Marva recognized it as Monte's pet. "I'm not sure if it's friendly, Trixie. Better just talk to it from here."

But the little girl touched her feet to the ground and started running. "Trixie!" Marva trotted after her with Ginny bouncing on her shoulder.

A throng of children, including Joey, had already gathered around the dog. Its tail whipped their legs as it tried to lick every face. When Trixie approached, the dog gave her a slurp from chin to forehead, and she sat down abruptly, knocked off balance. Marva expected her to cry, but instead she laughed in delight.

Although the dog seemed friendly enough, its increasing excitement worried Marva. It could unintentionally knock a small child flat. She bent over to catch Trixie's arm and pull her to a safe distance. The dog gave a little hop, and its warm tongue slopped over Marva's lips and cheek.

"Eeww! Eeww! Oh bleah!" She staggered back, wiping her sleeve across her face. The children laughed, entirely unsympathetic, and continued to pat the dog.

A shrill whistle split the air. The dog's ears pricked; its head cocked. An instant later it vaulted Trixie in one bound and swished past Marva's skirts.

She spun around to see Monte, Myles, and Beulah approaching, all three wearing wide smiles. The dog capered around Monte's feet, tongue lolling.

"Mama!" Trixie scrambled up and ran to greet Beulah, who scooped up her disheveled child.

"Are you hungry, sweetie pie? It's nearly time for supper."

"I hungry." Trixie pointed at the dog. "Dog."

"Yes, dear, it certainly is a dog. A rambunctious dog."

"Ralph loves children," Monte said quickly. "And pretty women." He met Marva's gaze, and she saw a twinkle in his eyes. He had definitely witnessed Ralph's display of affection.

"We'll have to clean up all these children before supper, but we'll meet you in the dining room," Myles told his brother. The two men thumped each other on the shoulders and parted ways. Monte and his dog headed toward the shore.

"I can't thank you enough for this, Marva," Beulah said as Myles took the fussing Ginny from Marva's arms. Joey clung to his father's leg and jabbered about dogs. Myles smoothed his son's sand-crusted forehead and smiled absently at his talk.

"Did you have a good talk with. . .with your brother?" She wasn't sure what to call him, though in her thoughts he was Monte.

"Very good," Myles said. "He's an amazing man. What a blessing to see the changes God has made in his life! And he's just as startled by the changes God has worked in me. The last he knew me, I was a bitter young man."

"How nice." Marva's arm felt weak and light, empty of Ginny's weight. A damp spot where the baby drooled on her shoulder felt cold. "I believe I'll go freshen up, too. See you at dinner."

What kind of friend was she to begrudge Myles and Beulah this special time with Monte? The children were not particularly difficult to watch.

To her surprise, Monte joined her on the path to the lodge. "I know Myles and Beulah have thanked you for watching their children these past few days, but I want to add my own thanks. You're a generous woman to give of your time for our benefit."

More guilt heaped on her conscience. "I'm glad I could help."

He held the door open for her. "Thank you," Marva said. In Monte Van Huysen's dark eyes, she read admiration, gratitude, and. . .something more?

"I'll see you at supper, Miss Obermeier."

An idea took shape in her mind. If she was ever to find Lucky, she needed to visit other lodges in the area. Members of the Lakeland Lodge staff must travel into town occasionally for supplies, mail, and news. Monte was a member of the staff. He probably ran errands for the lodge along with his guide duties. She could ask him for a ride and. . . Dreams of Monte's attentive company blotted thoughts of the elusive Lucky from her head.

In the hall outside her room, she stopped cold and clapped one hand over her face. *No! I am here in search of Lucky in Lakeland, and I must not allow myself to be distracted. I am through forever with chasing after men or even thinking about chasing after men! If Monte Van Huysen wants to be with me, he will have to do the chasing.*

❧

"Monte, have you got a minute?" Hardy Stowell burst into

Monte's office, nearly colliding with him in the doorway. His wispy hair stood on end like a wavering halo of gold around his head.

"Sure. What's wrong? Sit down before you collapse." Monte caught his friend by the shoulders and pushed him into a chair.

"Nothing is wrong! I wanted to tell you earlier, but your family was there. . . ." Hardy fanned his face with an envelope and rubbed his head. "She said she might walk with me after supper—Miss Obermeier did." His electrified hair sprang back out as soon as his hand passed over it.

"Oh. Really." Monte realized how flat his response sounded and tried again. "That's nice."

Hardy gave a little laugh.

"Don't get your hopes up too high," Monte warned in mild concern and a flash of jealousy.

Hardy shook his head and stood up. "I know. A woman like her wouldn't look twice at a fellow like me. I can't help wondering why she's never married. Bad disposition? Hard to believe with that angel face of hers. Domineering parents? Disappointment in her youth?"

"Hard to say," Monte responded after an empty pause. "I suppose you could ask her."

Hardy smiled, and his pale eyes shimmered. "If I have the courage."

After his partner left the office, Monte flopped into his desk chair and glared at the opposite wall.

❧

Everyone gathered in the lodge dining room for supper that evening, a fish fry of walleye and bluegill. Marva sat at her parents' table, enjoying her first quiet meal. George and Dorothy Hilbert, the newlyweds, joined them, chatting happily about their hiking excursion into the local woods. Above the murmur of conversation, Marva heard Trixie Van Huysen scream in garbled protest about something. She ate slightly faster in case Beulah might need her help.

Sensing a presence at her elbow, she looked up to meet Mr. Stowell's hopeful gaze. "Miss Obermeier?"

While chewing and swallowing a mouthful of fish, she patted her lips with her napkin and laid it on her plate. "Yes, sir?"

"I see you're not yet finished. I trust you still have the time and inclination to honor me with your presence this evening? To take a walk?"

"Oh." She glanced around at the Van Huysen table. Trixie perched on her uncle Monte's knee, playing with his string tie. The children appeared to be cheerful and cooperative. "Yes, I believe so. That would be nice, Mr. Stowell." Sensing his impatience, she decided to forgo dessert.

"There is no hurry. You may enjoy your meal while I visit other guests. Simply let me know when you're ready."

"Very well."

Mr. Stowell shook her father's hand and greeted her mother, then nodded to the Hilberts. The man had good manners; that was certain.

When Marva rose and brushed off her skirt, Mr. Stowell hurried across the room to join her. Everyone at the lodge must know by now that she had agreed to walk with him. With one hand at the back of her waist, he escorted her from the dining room. As they passed the Van Huysens' table, Beulah looked up and gave her a knowing smile. Monte remained focused on his nieces and nephews.

Evening light lingered over the lake. "Shall we stroll down to the shore, or would you prefer an actual walk?" Mr. Stowell asked. "The dragonflies are out in vast numbers tonight to protect us from mosquitoes."

"How thoughtful of them," Marva said with a smile. "I think I should like to take some exercise after that meal."

"As you wish." He offered his arm, and Marva looped her hand through the crook of his elbow. They fell into step, following the wagon track away from the lake.

"Tell me about yourself, Miss Obermeier. Why has such a lovely woman never married? Or am I too bold?" His voice sounded tight with nerves.

"The answer is simple enough. The right man has never asked me." Marva felt calm and composed. "Why are you unmarried, Mr. Stowell?"

"I was married once."

"Did your wife pass?"

A pause. "Yes, she is dead." His tone discouraged further questions, which seemed unfair to Marva.

"I'm sorry. How long has it been?" Hearing a high-pitched whine, she waved at her ear.

"A few years. Do you wish to marry, Miss Obermeier, or do you intend to remain single?"

Irritation prickled. "I would marry if the right opportunity arose." She gazed up at his taut profile. "Do you ever read the *Longtree Enquirer*, Mr. Stowell?"

He gave her a puzzled look. "The what?"

"It is our local newspaper. Your lodge advertises in it, which is how our group came to be here. I merely wondered if you ever read the paper." Now a fly buzzed into her face; she swatted it away.

He looked thoughtful. "Now that you mention it, yes, I believe I have seen a copy lying around the lodge upon occasion."

She decided to take the plunge. "Have you ever written a

personal note to the *Longtree Enquirer*, sir? In answer to an advertisement or some such thing?"

"I have not." He licked his lips and looked uncomfortable. "Might I inquire as to where these questions lead, Miss Obermeier?"

"I wish to locate a person who has been communicating with me through the newspaper; that is all. It is unimportant, Mr. Stowell."

Now that she knew he bore no connection to "Lucky in Lakeland," Marva was eager to return to the lodge and escape his company. "Ooh, the insects are dreadful this evening." She slapped her arm, and her hand felt sticky with her own blood. "I do not think the dragonflies are doing their job properly after all."

"Perhaps if we strolled down beside the water where there is a breeze—"

"I think we had better take cover, Mr. Stowell, but thank you anyway." Her pace nearly doubled on the way back.

His face revealed disappointment when she bade him farewell at the lodge's front door. "Such a pleasant stroll. Thank you again."

Once back in the small suite she shared with her parents, she picked up a certain book from her father's bedside table and found her place. The lurid cover art no longer amused her; she was entirely engrossed in the adventurous, slightly romantic tale of the Wild West. She read the book only when her parents were not around. There was no point in advertising her foolish interest in its author.

Sometime later, a loon's call startled her back to reality. The bird sounded close. Although she knew quite well that she would not see it from the window, she rose to pull aside the curtain.

A moonlit path shimmered on the lake, so lovely that tears pooled in Marva's eyes at the sight. Such a night was meant for lovers. But God had given it to her, as well, and she would not let His gift go to waste.

❧

Monte scribbled out a new scene while listening for his partner's return, but his gaze kept returning to the clock. Focusing with an effort, he shuffled through his pages. His fictional hero seemed to him hapless and idiotic: The Sioux braves who had trapped the "idiot" alone in a gully behaved more like children than like genuine warriors, the "idiot's" romance with the widow of a settler had fizzled with no conceivable hope of renewal, and even the "idiot's" mustang behaved like an oversized hound dog. Who would want to read such twaddle? Monte jabbed his pen into its holder and shoved back his chair.

Rising, he paced across his office and stared out the dark window. Moonlight glittered on the lake. Were Hardy and Marva enjoying the sight together? Could a beautiful woman like Miss Obermeier find a man like Hardy appealing? Stranger things had happened. After all, Hardy was a good fellow in his way. It may be that he and Marva had discovered soul mates in each other. They might talk for hours and never run out of topics. They might enjoy a comfortable silence and drink in the beauty of the night, arm in arm. Even hand in hand, if the romance progressed rapidly.

No, surely not. Marva seemed too reserved for that kind of familiarity. But maybe she was only reserved with Monte. Maybe with other men she could relax and laugh. Beulah had said something once about Marva's reputation for talking nonstop. Why did she seem constrained and uncomfortable in Monte's presence? Was it because he talked too much and overwhelmed her? Was it because she sensed his physical attraction to her?

He pulled out his watch and glared at its face. The burning heaviness in his chest revealed more about his feelings than he wanted to know. *Lord, when will I learn to be content with reality?*

Just when he thought he had finally outgrown his weaknesses, just when he was ready to settle down in a prosaic marriage with a desperate-yet-steady spinster, just then, Miss Marva Obermeier stepped off the train and knocked him emotionally sprawling. Here he was, forty years of age yet still easy prey to temptations of the flesh and the heart. Who would have thought that his steady, godly, mature correspondent would turn out to be the kind of woman he had always dreamed about?

But then. . .what if he was wrong about Miss Obermeier being his newspaper lady? He was 98 percent sure, but that remaining 2 percent loomed large in his mind despite his attempts to ignore it.

Real life never resembled fiction. . .did it?

six

The heavens declare the glory of God;
and the firmament sheweth his handywork.
Day unto day uttereth speech,
and night unto night sheweth knowledge.
PSALM 19:1-2

Monte shoved the watch back into his pocket and leaned on the windowsill. His eyes opened wide; then he jutted his chin forward and squinted in disbelief. Was he seeing things?

Silvery moonlight gleamed on the pale hair of a lone figure seated on the end of the dock. Monte saw no one else nearby, although a person could be hidden from his view by intervening trees. Squinting and trying to peer around these brushy obstacles, he searched for. . . For what? His rival? Why was he behaving like a jealous schoolboy?

The sound of a familiar, hacking cough almost stopped his heart. Immediately he stepped across the hall and knocked on the door of the office that connected to Hardy's sleeping quarters. No answer. He knocked harder.

"What is it?" Hardy growled. "I'm in bed. Go away."

"When did you get back? I've been waiting to talk to you."

More coughing. "I got back before you did. Can't it wait until morning? I'm tired."

He was heartless, no doubt, to feel cheered by the depressed tone of his friend's voice, but Monte couldn't stop his reaction. "All right. See you then."

He quickly closed up his office and left the lodge. A few guests lingered in rocking chairs on the long veranda facing the lake. He returned their greetings and hurried on toward the lakeshore.

His steps slowed gradually, and his breathing became short. There she was, still perched on the end of the dock. With hair like spun starlight, it could be no one but Marva Obermeier. He heard water splashing as she swung her feet.

As soon as his boots touched the dock, she turned her head to look at him.

"Mind if I join you?" he asked softly. "It's a perfect night."

She faced back toward the lake, her shoulders stiff. "I have no claim on the dock, Mr. Van Huysen." Her shoes made a dark mound on the boards behind her.

"No, but you do have a say about whether or not a man sits beside you. I promise to be quiet if you're craving peace." He proceeded to the end of the dock.

She braced her palms on either side of herself but made no move to rise. He sat nearby yet not too close. "Is the water warm?"

"It's nice." Her voice was so quiet he had to strain to hear.

"I'd take off my boots and dangle my feet, except I'm afraid the stink of my feet would chase you away."

She laughed, a quick snort and chuckle. "I'm not that sensitive, Mr. Van Huysen. My papa keeps pigs. I doubt your feet could smell worse than their sty on a summer night."

"You might be surprised."

Monte untied his boots and removed them and his socks, one after another. The cool water gave his feet a shock at first, but within moments, he scarcely felt the chill. Happiness filled him so full that some of it had to escape in a deep sigh.

"A busy day?" she asked, back to that polite and formal tone.

"No busier than usual. Tomorrow I've got to make a run into town."

She looked at him with evident interest. "May I come along? I have. . .inquiries to make."

Inquiries? His thoughts raced ahead. "If it's not impertinent to ask, what kind of inquiries must you make? Perhaps I might be of assistance."

She clasped her hands in her lap and studied them. Monte simply watched her, enjoying the view.

"I need to find out about resort lodges in the area. I need to. . .to meet their owners."

Monte rubbed his hand over his mouth to hide his smile. "You're dissatisfied with Lakeland Lodge?"

She shook her head. "Not at all. This is another matter. A private matter. I spoke with Mr. Stowell today, and he told me that several local lodges are owned by unmarried gentlemen."

"I can think of a few. Why must the owners be unmarried?"

"That is not your business, Mr. Van Huysen."

He turned his face away until he could keep amusement out of his voice. "Tell you what: After I pick up the mail and supplies, I'll drive you around to some local lodges. We'll make up a list, and you tell me which ones you want to visit."

When she turned to look at him, her face was in shadow. "Do you really have time for that?"

"It would be my pleasure, Miss Obermeier. At Lakeland Lodge, guests always come first." He gave a little seated bow. "If you don't object to a personal observation, I'd say that you need a break from my nieces and nephews for at least one day."

When she said nothing, he continued. "I admire how you help Beulah with her children. She can't praise you highly enough, to my way of thinking."

"They're dear children."

"I agree, yet even the dearest children get tiring. You must have patience beyond the lot of mortals. From the Lord, that is."

She laughed again. "I get wearier and crankier than anyone knows, because if I expressed my frustration, everyone would know the real me—and I can't let that happen!"

Although she spoke in jest, he heard the note of truth in her words. "Aren't we all that way—hiding our real selves from the world? But the good thing about it is that we can sympathize with one another. I still admire the fact that you keep up a cheery front—put on a brave face."

She gazed out across the lake, moonlight turning her features to marble. "If I were truly brave and cheery, it wouldn't have to be a front. I know I should trust God and be grateful for the life He has given me, but instead of being content, I doubt His wisdom and try to force change into my life."

Startled by this sudden glimpse into her soul, he pondered an equally honest reply. "My method of doubting Him is more along the lines of being afraid to attempt changes."

Silence fell between them. Monte could think of nothing more to say, yet he wanted to prolong the moment.

She turned around and picked up her shoes. "What time do you plan to leave for town in the morning, Mr. Van Huysen?"

"Not till after breakfast." He rose and helped her up. Her hand felt cool and strong in his. "I'll bring the wagon around in front of the lodge."

"Then I'll see you in the morning." She smiled briefly at him and walked toward the shore, her footsteps nearly silent on the dock. He hoped her bare feet wouldn't pick up splinters.

❧

"But Marva, I don't understand why you feel this need to go into town. I disapprove of an unmarried woman riding around this wilderness land with an unmarried man, even if he is Myles's brother."

Marva tucked a wisp of hair back into her bun and picked at her breakfast pancakes with a fork. "I simply wish to make a few inquiries around town, Mother, and there is nothing indiscreet about sitting beside a man in an open wagon."

Papa cleared his throat. His beard bobbled back and forth as he chewed. He swallowed and said, "I believe your mother is asking what kind of inquiries you intend to make. I confess a curiosity along those lines myself."

Marva met his direct gaze and acknowledged herself defeated. "Never mind. It isn't important anyway. But I do believe I am old enough to travel about unescorted without setting too many tongues wagging."

"Not with a handsome man like Monte Van Huysen, you're not," Mother said with uncharacteristic shortness. Marva sensed her parents' displeasure at her refusal to explain, but she wasn't about to deceive them, and neither would she tell them the truth.

Now that she thought the matter over objectively, she realized how awkward it would be to interview lodge owners with Monte Van Huysen hovering in the background, possibly nosing into her personal business. And if she were to find Lucky, he might well object to her coming to meet him in the company of another eligible bachelor. Her parents' objection was probably for the best.

She asked for Monte at the front desk but was told that he had already left his office. "You might find him at the stables, ma'am."

"And the stables are. . . ?"

The grizzled desk clerk pointed straight at the door, then jerked his finger to one side. "Quickest way is out the lodge door, turn left, and follow the path until you see the stables."

After hurrying back to the dining room to tell her parents where she was going, she started her quest. The lodge grounds were quiet at this hour. A doe and her spotted twin fawns crossed the path ahead of her, stopped to stare, and then trotted on into the underbrush. A woodpecker hammered somewhere overhead, but Marva couldn't spot it.

She soon saw weathered buildings in a clearing. From the confines of a large corral, a mule and several horses observed her approach with mild interest. The distinctive odors of horse and hay mingled with the scent of pine.

As she rounded a bend, she saw Monte Van Huysen in front of a carriage house, harnessing a horse. The animal pricked its ears and snuffled at her approach, and Monte turned to follow its gaze. Seeing her, he straightened and brushed off his hands. "Miss Obermeier."

"Good morning, Mr. Van Huysen. I came to tell you that I will not be able to go to town with you today after all." She couldn't help but be pleased to see his evident disappointment. "My parents disapprove of the idea. Mother thinks it unseemly for me to ride alone with you into town, which I think is ridiculous, but I cannot change her mind."

"They're welcome to come along with us."

She shook her head. "That wouldn't work, but thank you anyway."

"Maybe another day?"

"I—I don't think so."

He sighed. "All the anticipation just drained out of this day, Petunia, old girl." He addressed the words to his horse. Marva smiled in amusement.

"Do you enjoy fishing?" he asked, giving her a look from the corner of his eye.

"Sometimes. I used to enjoy it anyway."

He took a step closer. "I'm taking your father out tomorrow morning. You could come along. . .if you wanted to. You haven't truly experienced the Northwoods until you've been out on the lake early on a summer morning."

"I might just do that. Thank you. Have a good trip today, Mr. Van Huysen."

She felt his gaze follow as she walked away, head high, shoulders back.

But finding Lucky should be her focus. Frustration with her own weakness for a handsome man increased her determination. Somehow, one way or another, she must visit neighboring lodges. Time was slipping past, and soon her chance would be gone. If she did not make an opportunity, no one would.

Mr. Stowell rose politely and smiled when she entered his office.

"Please, Mr. Stowell, could you arrange for me to borrow a horse and cart?"

He gripped the back of his office chair. Standing with his shoulders against the wall, he seemed to use his desk like a shield against her influence. "I would be pleased to drive you anywhere you wish to go."

"Thank you kindly, but no, I would not feel right about dragging you away from your work. I am an able driver."

She at last wangled a promise from him that she might have use of a horse and dogcart Thursday morning. He still seemed uneasy, but he did agree.

"Thank you ever so much! I appreciate this more than you can know, Mr. Stowell. You are a gem and a true friend."

"Am I?" His face flushed.

"I can harness and hitch a horse by myself," she offered.

"That won't be necessary. Our boys will ready one for you. At nine o'clock?"

"Ideal! I shall be there. Oh! One more thing—do you have a map of the area, and might you be willing to mark on it the locations of the nearest vacation lodges?"

He appeared bewildered. "A map? I don't know the area all that well. Mr. Van Huysen would be better able to assist you in that way."

"Mr. Van Huysen? I would prefer he not know about my venture. I wish you would please do it." She used her most persuasive tone and blinked sweetly.

"I'll—Well, I'll try."

Something in his tone informed her that he remained wary.

seven

Not by works of righteousness which we have done,
but according to his mercy he saved us,
by the washing of regeneration, and renewing of the Holy Ghost;
which he shed on us abundantly through Jesus Christ our Saviour.
TITUS 3:5-6

"Take my hand—careful now." Marva gripped Monte's hand and stepped cautiously into the small fishing boat. Papa took her other hand and helped guide her to the small bench set in the bow. She turned in time to see Monte release her skirt from a splinter on the gunwale while Papa rescued a bucket of bait from overturning.

"I'm sorry. I hope this wasn't a bad idea, my coming along today." She knew she had made them get a late start. The rosy pink in the eastern sky was already fading to silver blue, and sunlight peeked through the treetops across the lake.

Papa made a noncommittal little grunt. Monte loaded a tackle box, untied the boat from the dock, and hopped in. Just before he started rowing, he glanced back at Marva over one shoulder and winked. "A woman aboard ship may be bad luck, but we'll take the risk." He turned to her father. "Would you please shove us off?"

Marva turned forward, letting the moist morning air brush her face. No breeze disturbed the lake's mirror surface. With each stroke of the oars, the little boat surged forward. Just beneath the water's green surface she saw the tops of water weeds and an occasional fish.

"Right around here is where the reverend and I caught those walleye the other day," Papa said from his seat in the boat's stern after Monte had rowed a good distance.

"This is a good spot," Monte said. "Want to drop anchor here and give it a try?"

"Why not?"

Marva heard him ship oars as quietly as possible. The anchor made a little splash when he slipped it over the side. She tipped her head over the bow and stared down into the dark water, straining her eyes to glimpse a fish.

"You'll catch more fish with a pole and some bait, Marva-girl," Papa said in mild reproof. She turned with a smile and had to shade her eyes. Morning sun reflected off the water with almost unbearable brilliance.

"Good thing you wore that sun hat. It's going to be a hot day," Monte remarked.

Marva adjusted her hat's broad brim. "I do burn easily. You don't share your brother's complexion, I notice."

"I was lucky. Our mother was a redhead like Myles. I got my hair and complexion from our father, though I burn more easily than he did." He adjusted his cap. "Still need a hat on a day like this, though. No sense in taking chances."

The two men were already baiting hooks and adjusting their lines. Marva disliked impaling minnows or worms; she preferred artificial bait even if nothing bit at it. Smoothing her skirt, she allowed herself to watch Monte. So active and strong. Gray sprinkled the hair at his temples, and his face was lined from squinting into the sun. . .or maybe from smiling. This evidence of age was comforting rather than repelling, since her own face and form were beginning to show signs of wear.

He turned to straddle his bench and gave her a sideways look. "I dug beetle grubs out of a rotted log last night. Sometimes I have luck with them. Want me to bait your line?"

She nodded. "Thank you."

"Always tried to break the girl of squeamishness," her father said regretfully. "Never could get her to bait her own hooks."

Monte chuckled. "Gives us men a purpose—hook baiters." He handed her the pole with the squirming grub swinging from the end of its line. "Know how to cast?"

She nodded and concentrated on taking the pole without hitting herself or anyone else in the face with the grub. Monte slowly released his hold and sat back to watch her cast. The grub sailed smoothly through the air and hit the water's surface with a tiny *plop* a good distance away.

"Nice cast."

"Thank you." Marva returned his smile.

Soon the three of them sat and watched their bobbers. A bald eagle soared near the shore and landed in a dead tree, studying them with its head turned to one side. Marva could see its yellow beak and ruffled feathers.

Monte sat with his feet propped on the edge of the boat, leaning his elbows on his knees. She heard him humming softly but couldn't catch the tune. He reeled in his line, grumbled over stolen bait, and cast again.

"Look over there."

Marva followed Monte's pointing finger and saw a V-shaped ripple moving near the shore. "What is it?"

"I'd guess it's a muskrat. We had a family of minks nesting on our shore two years back. They cleaned out all the muskrats and chipmunks. But then the minks moved on, so the little critters are coming back."

Papa caught a small bass, too small to keep. He baited his

hook with a minnow and tried again on the other side of the boat.

The sun's heat began to penetrate Marva's hat and her blue cotton gown. She shifted uncomfortably and thought about taking off her shoes. *Oh, to be a carefree child again!*

A breeze sent ripples over the lake's surface, making the boat gently rock and spin in a lazy circle around its anchor chain. Marva leaned her arm on the side of the boat and rested her head on it. Sunlight trickled through the weave of her hat. She closed her eyes, waving off a fly.

Sometime later she stirred, dimly realizing that she had dozed off. Something brushed against her side, and she started up. "Oh!"

Monte was kneeling on the floorboards beside her seat, holding her wildly bending and pulling fishing pole. He glanced down and saw that she was awake. "You got one, Marva! Hurry up, take the pole and reel it in!" He grabbed her hand and shoved the pole into her nerveless fingers. Still dazed, she couldn't seem to grasp it properly, so he helped her, his hand over hers on the reel, his other arm reaching around her to steady the pole. His touch served only to increase her ineptitude. "There he is! We've got him now!" The fish's silvery sides flashed in the sunlight as it made a wild leap into the air.

Monte half stood in the teetering rowboat, his chest pressed against the back of Marva's head, his hands reaching for the line. "Get the net, Mr. Obermeier! Hurry!"

Papa scrambled to hand him the net and moved Monte's pole out of the way.

Leaning far over the side of the boat, Monte reached for the fish as it dangled from the end of the line. Water sloshed into the bottom of the boat. Marva tried to hold the pole steady, but the fish flipped and struggled.

"Easy! Reel him in a bit farther."

"I'm trying to. He's heavy!" Finally the netted fish lay in the bottom of the boat.

"A magnificent walleye! What a fish! Congratulations, Miss Obermeier, you are the fisherwoman of the day!" He sat beside her on the narrow bench and gave her shoulders a squeeze. The walleye lay on the floorboards, gasping for breath. Marva felt like gasping for breath, too.

"Isn't he a pretty fish?" A brainless comment, yet she didn't know what else to say or do. Did Monte know what he was doing to her?

Papa seemed entirely unaware of his daughter's reactions. He and Monte both crowed over the fish and praised Marva to the skies.

On the pretext of examining her catch more closely, Marva bent over, out of Monte's casual grasp, and reached out to touch the fish's slimy side. It gave a final, violent flop. Startled and nervous, she sat up with a jerk, coming halfway to her feet just as Monte started to rise. Her head connected solidly with his jaw.

"Ow!" His cry blended with hers. Grabbing the top of her head, she sat down hard, nearly missing the bench. The boat rocked wildly. Amid scrabbling thumps and startled exclamations from both men, a bait bucket turned over and doused Marva's feet with flopping minnows and smelly water. Squealing, she jumped up again, lost her balance, and dropped back to her seat.

Splash! Water cascaded into the pitching boat as Monte back flopped over the side. Marva and her father stared, openmouthed, Marva clutching the top of her head. Her hat dangled over her shoulder. Minnows skittered around her feet in a good inch of lake water.

Monte surfaced, wiped water from his face, and wiggled his jaw back and forth. "All these years as a fishing guide, and this is the first time I took a plunge."

"Are you all right, Mr. Van Huysen? I'm terribly sorry!"

"Nothing permanently damaged—except my pride. Balance the boat, please. I'm coming aboard." He pulled himself over the side, dumping another wave into the bottom of the boat in the process.

"We've taken on water," Papa said in vast understatement. "Better do some bailing out." He used a tin cup as a scoop.

"We're starting our own onboard aquarium," Marva observed, watching minnows dart around her feet. Even her walleye looked somewhat encouraged by the rising water level. She started scooping water over the side with her cupped hands.

Meanwhile, Monte hauled off his boots and emptied them over the side. His socks were holey, Marva noticed. Using one of the oars, he fished his floating hat from the water and plopped it on the bench.

He met Marva's gaze and began to chuckle. She smiled but felt dangerously close to tears.

He reached out one big, wet hand to squeeze her arm and gave her a wink. "Guess I needed cooling off anyway."

Did he intend some double meaning? He laughed again, pushing his dripping hair straight back from his forehead. Taking another cup, he helped bail, rounding up minnows and returning them to their bucket. With all of them working, the water level inside the boat eventually dropped.

She tried not to grimace while Monte strung a line through her walleye's gills and lowered it over the side. "I always feel so sorry for the poor fish once they're caught."

"Nonsense," Monte said. "He'll be delicious once he's fried."

At that moment, Marva's father gave his pole a jerk and eagerly started reeling in another fish. Monte hurried to assist him, just as he had helped Marva. She wanted to kick herself for being so stupid, so susceptible, overreacting to Monte's touch the way she had. He must find her amusing in a pathetic sort of way.

To Marva's relief, the men decided to end the outing early, since sitting around in soggy clothes wasn't Monte's idea of a good time. He rowed them back to the landing and helped Marva climb ashore before he unloaded any of the gear. "Wait," he said, clambering up after her. "Miss Obermeier, please don't feel bad about my. . .uh. . .swim today. It wasn't your fault. I was hovering too close and got what I had coming." He dropped his gaze, then grinned up at her with his chin still lowered. "I've never been fishing guide to a beautiful woman before. Guess I found out what not to do."

❧

Ralph came rushing to meet Monte halfway to his cabin. Tongue lolling, the dog frisked about, stopped to sniff his master's wet trousers, and then burst back into wild frolicking. Monte watched Ralph's antics with a fond smile. "Oh, to have such energy and enthusiasm again."

He was hoping to escape observance and comment by avoiding the main path, but no such luck. "Mr. Van Huysen, what happened to you?" a female voice called.

He turned to see a cluster of women on the trail up to the lodge. Every eye was turned upon him. He recognized Marva's mother in the mix.

"I fell into the lake," he said with a wave of his limp hat. "Have a nice luncheon, ladies." Before they could question him further, he hurried off, shivering.

"Foolishness," he muttered while standing on the uneven

floorboards in the middle of the cabin's main room, stripping off his wet garments. "I acted like a fool kid. She probably thinks. . . No telling what she thinks. I'm too old for such foolishness."

Grimacing and growling, he continued to berate himself while donning fresh garments and hanging the wet ones over his clothesline hung between two pines. The daunting prospect of facing curious people in the lodge dining room prompted him to rummage through his own poorly stocked cupboards. A can of pork and beans made an unappetizing meal, but at least it stopped his stomach from growling.

He stepped out on the porch with Ralph at his heels, leaned on the railing, and stared through intervening branches at the glittering lake. After a moment's thought, he shook his head and closed his eyes, wanting to pray but unable to put a request into words.

What to do? Thinking back over the morning, he could make nothing of Mr. Obermeier's comments and reactions from the day's adventure. Was the old man aware of Monte's attraction to his daughter? Did he approve or disapprove? That bland German face of his revealed nothing except good humor. Monte thumped his palm on the railing.

And Mrs. Obermeier was no easier to read. Mild and friendly, she seemed sweetly oblivious to any emotional undercurrents.

But then, how did he want them to react? What would he do if Mr. Obermeier came calling to inquire about Monte's intentions toward Marva? If she were eighteen and he were twenty-one, that might be the natural course of events. But now? He had much to offer a woman as far as material possessions were concerned, and all honestly gained.

If only he had not made such a hash of his life back in those early days. A woman like Marva would recoil from him if she knew his past. How could she not? But for God's grace, he would be long since dead, a dried-up corpse hanging from a cottonwood tree on the plains of Texas.

But for God's grace. Because of Christ's cleansing blood, he was no longer a hopeless sinner. When God looked at Montague Van Huysen, He saw a man clothed in His Son's righteousness, sanctified and holy.

God looks on the heart. However, man looks on the outward appearance, and a man's past had a way of haunting him throughout life on this earth.

Again Monte shook his head and sighed. Yet even while he headed to his office to catch up on paperwork, part of his mind calculated where Marva might be at this hour.

❧

"Certainly, Hardy." Monte leaned back in his chair and peered over the tops of his reading glasses. "Are you planning to spy on our competition?"

Hardy frowned. "No. This is for a lodger who requested a map of the area."

"For what purpose?"

"I was not informed. Does it matter?"

Monte lifted his brows and tapped the map with his knuckles. "It might. Although we warn our guests about the hazards of wandering unescorted in these woods, there are always some who scoff at danger."

"The main roads are safe in daylight hours."

"That depends on which roads, which hours, and which traveler, I should say. Hardy, is this map intended for Miss Obermeier?"

His partner's blush was answer enough.

"I see. And you intend to accompany her?"

"She turned down my escort. I promised her the dogcart,"

Hardy mumbled under his breath and fidgeted.

"All right. I'll take care of it."

"But she's expecting me to provide the map. She. . .uh. . . didn't want you to know about it."

"You will provide the map, and for all she knows, I remain in ignorance. As soon as I finish marking it, I'll leave it on your desk. What time did you order the dogcart?"

"For 9:00 a.m. tomorrow."

Monte bent over the map. "Very well. I'll be running errands myself tomorrow, so I'll do what I can to make sure Miss Obermeier comes to no grief."

Hardy's worried expression vanished. "Good. I didn't want to have to follow her around. At least now I know why she never married. She may be beautiful, but she's far too bossy."

After his office door closed behind Hardy's back, Monte chuckled, quieted and thought a moment, and then laughed aloud.

eight

Boast not thyself of to morrow;
for thou knowest not what a day may bring forth.
PROVERBS 27:1

Morning sunlight dappled the road and the horse and Marva's hands on the reins. She gazed up, way up, at shimmering golden green leaves arching over her like the high roof of a cathedral. Blending with the *squeak* of leather, the *clank* and *whir* of metal, and the *clip-clop* of hooves was the clamor of birdsong from every side. A flock of some kind of chirping bird must have settled in this particular patch of trees, for their chatter was nearly deafening.

Her horse, a wiry brown gelding with a sour expression, answered to the name of Buzz according to the stable boy. So far his nature seemed sweeter than his looks indicated, for he trotted along willingly enough.

Marva studied her map, frowning. It was difficult to judge how far she had traveled along the dotted line indicating Lakeland Lodge's driveway, but the main east-west highway, Lac du Flambeau Road, should appear ahead soon. According to Hardy Stowell, the drive to Johnson Lake would take little more than an hour. From there she intended to drive over to another lodge on Brandy Lake, then head home. Taken at an easy pace, the outing should take no more than five or six hours, depending on how much time she spent at each lodge.

Should she locate Lucky in Lakeland. . . Well, in that case, her calculations might fall through. She drew a deep breath and wriggled her shoulders in an attempt to relax.

Somehow, when she had pictured coming north to search the area for Lucky, her mind had failed to grasp the enormity and the wildness of this lake country. Interviewing local lodge owners had seemed like a straightforward proposition back then. Perhaps if she were a man and acquainted with the lay of the land, she might have visited every lodge in five counties within three weeks. Ha! Maybe not.

She had also failed to consider how awkward it would be to ask about unmarried lodge owners. Why did people have to be so nosy?

But perseverance and ingenuity had paid off. She hoped. Her parents had plans for the day; if all went smoothly, she should be back before they so much as noticed her absence.

Yet, even after all this effort, she still might find no sign of Lucky.

Actually, in all likelihood, her efforts would come to naught.

"Lord," she prayed aloud, "I know I'm bullheaded as can be, but You've opened this door for me, so I'm asking You to bless my efforts. Please let me find Lucky today and bring some answers to my questions! If he is not the man You want me to marry, then I guess You'll say no, but I would really appreciate knowing Your reasons why or why not."

The forest suddenly opened up onto a road still shadowed by trees. Buzz turned right without any command from Marva and picked up his pace. A fresh breeze cooled her face until she shivered slightly. Trying to hold her map still, she checked her next turn.

A small bridge ahead spanned a stream or small river. Buzz laid back his ears when his feet hit its echoing timbers, and when the cart's wheels rumbled, he bolted into a canter; but

Marva quickly brought him back into control. With the bridge behind, he settled back into his quick trot, ears twitching.

"Testing me, were you?" she commented.

He snorted, appearing to ignore her.

A doe and her fawn grazed on the roadside ahead. Heads lifted, ears pricked, they watched the horse and cart approaching. Turning his head in their direction, Buzz looked at them and whinnied. Immediately their tails lifted and they bounded into the trees.

"I think you've been rejected, Buzz," Marva commented.

A wagon appeared on the road ahead, tiny in the distance. At the sight, Marva's heart picked up its pace. Of course, she could be in no real danger; this was settled country, after all.

Two Indian men, one young, one with gray hair, occupied the approaching wagon. They studied Marva with impassive stares, returned her polite nod as the vehicles passed on the road, and traveled on west. She heaved a sigh of relief, waving dust away from her face.

The road ahead forked. "Whoa." Buzz stopped, champing at his bit and snorting softly. A hand-painted signpost with three branches read: *Woodruff*, *Squirrel Lake Rd.*, and *Merrill*. The tilted post indicated points midway between the three roads. She wanted Trout Lake Road. Confusion formed a lump in her chest. She looked from her map to the roads but saw no correlation. Had she somehow managed to miss the highway? Was she at some crossroads not even located on her map?

At last she decided to take the right fork, which seemed to lead straight ahead. If only she were a better judge of direction. . .

Within fifteen minutes she knew she had made the wrong choice. Or had she? A lake appeared on her right, but it appeared to be small, nothing like the large lake on her map. At last she reined in Buzz and sat staring straight ahead. "I'm lost." There was nothing to do but go back, which meant turning her horse around. Rather than attempt turning Buzz on the narrow road, she climbed down and went to his head. He allowed her to turn him until the dogcart faced back along the road she had just traveled, but as soon as she let go of his bridle, he trotted quickly away. "Whoa!" In a panic, she chased the cart along the road, but the horse rapidly outdistanced her. Would he run all the way back to the lodge?

❧

Monte saw Buzz and the empty dogcart approaching at a rapid clip. Marva must have realized her mistake and tried to turn around, and Buzz had played a prank on her. Stupid horse.

He turned Petunia sideways to block the road and called softly to the runaway. "Whoa, Buzzard Bait, you rotten beast, you." The gelding pricked his ears, slowed, and turned off to graze on the verge as if he had never intended to run home. Monte dismounted, watching the back trail for signs of Marva. If possible, he preferred to keep her unaware of his presence, since she was certain to resent it. He decided to wait in hiding on the assumption that she was unhurt. Buzz was not a vicious beast, just ornery at times.

He had to admit: *Like his owner.*

❧

Flies bombarded Marva whenever she stopped to pant, so she pressed on until a stitch developed in her side and sweat dampened her shirtwaist. A brisk walk while wearing a corset was pure misery, and the thought of the miles of road between her and the lodge deepened her woe. She removed her stylish suit jacket and felt slightly cooler, but she still could not draw a full breath. She must have been out of her mind to attempt this trek on her own in a strange place.

But then, rounding the road's slight bend to the right, she

saw Buzz ahead, grazing contentedly at the side of the road. He lifted his head and pricked his ears in her direction, gave a derisive little snort, and then ripped up another mouthful of grass. She approached the horse cautiously, talking in her calmest tone and hoping he wouldn't sense her anxiety.

He allowed her to catch him and lead him back to the road, and he stood quietly while she climbed into the dogcart. Relieved, she thanked God for His intervention on her behalf.

Soon she once again headed east, having lost nearly an hour from her time schedule. An unmarked track on her left caused her to stop and study her map again. Surely that could not be the road she wanted. . .or could it? Taking her chances, she forged on ahead. As she passed lakes not marked on her map, fear built in her chest. *Where am I? Lord, please help me!* A crossroad appeared ahead. This might be Trout Lake Road, although it did not look the way it was marked on her map. She turned left.

The forest on either side of the road gave way to clear-cut spaces and farms, resembling farmlands much farther south, although the houses and barns looked quite new. At another fork in the road, she saw a sign for the town of Woodruff. Stopping Buzz once more, she studied her map and realized that she had traveled far out of the way.

However, if she turned left here and passed through Woodruff, she could turn left again just north of town and reconnect with the road she had missed, making her way to the lodge on Johnson Lake. The knot inside her chest eased slightly. At least she now had some idea where she was.

Woodruff resembled Minocqua in its rough-hewn timber construction and appeared to be a thriving town. New construction met her gaze on all sides. Several horsemen and a few buggies and wagons occupied the streets. She saw only two women and a few children, but many men of all ages. Her passage through town garnered more interest than she desired. One man whooped out a comment, which she mercifully could not decipher.

Once more, she seriously doubted the wisdom of this solo endeavor. But then again, whom could she have brought along? Not either of her parents, certainly. And Beulah was far too busy with her children.

The road crossed railroad tracks, then turned left, which would be west, she figured. Hardy had drawn a dotted line indicating a turnoff to the—she squinted at the map—Northwoods Oasis, owned and operated by Mel Hendricks of Milwaukee.

Buzz's trot had slowed. She clucked and jiggled the reins. He laid back his ears but picked up his pace again. Buildings became scattered, and fences marked pastureland and fields. Did crops grow well here? The growing season must be short this far north.

Where was that lake? Stumps dotting many of the surrounding fields indicated that the area had been clear-cut for lumber. Marva had expected more shade during this drive. Her wide-brimmed hat kept direct sunlight off her head. She had decided against wearing driving gloves because they stung her hands, which had sunburned slightly on the lake the day before. A poor choice, she realized now that it was too late. The tops of her hands were mottled red and white and felt like fire.

Sweat trickled down her temples and between her shoulder blades. Who would have thought it would be so hot and humid today? She slipped one hand beneath her hat. Her hair was nearly hot enough to scorch her fingers.

She shaded the map with her hat and looked again for directions. The images blurred before her eyes. She fanned herself with the map and hunted for her canteen. Where was it? Had it fallen from the cart? Had she even put it into the cart that morning? Of all things to lose! But never mind. Once she arrived at the Northwoods Oasis lodge, she would surely be offered a cool drink and a chair in the shade.

Buzz must be suffering from the heat, too. Sweat foamed between his hind legs and darkened his shoulders. She should have stopped to get him a drink when they passed through Woodruff. If not for all those staring men, she might have thought of it.

According to Hardy's map, the turnoff should be someplace along here. She watched for a wagon track, for a post—anything to mark the place. At last she saw a track—shade at last! This area had retained most of its trees, probably for the sake of the resort.

Buzz shook his head as she asked him to turn, and he dropped to a walk; but he willingly stepped from the main road onto the shady, bumpy track. When a lake appeared ahead, the horse seemed to gaze at it longingly and snorted. "I'm sure you must be very thirsty, Buzz, and though I'm terribly sorry, we can't leave the track to get you a drink. Be patient a few minutes more, and we'll be at the lodge."

The horse walked on, his head bobbing with each stride. Once he turned his head to look back over one shoulder and neighed. Marva thought she heard a horse neigh in reply, but when she turned around, she saw nothing. The forest had closed in behind them.

At last a house came into view. If it could be called a house. Marva frowned and looked back at her map. This couldn't be a resort—it was a mere hovel built of unpeeled logs—and yet the track ended here.

A dog barked savagely from the end of its chain. The cabin door opened, and a hulking, unshaven man stepped outside with a rifle gripped in his hands. "Lady, you don't belong here."

"I'm looking for the Northwoods Oasis," she said.

"This ain't it."

"Oh. I'm sorry to have bothered you." She urged Buzz to turn. He bent his neck around and took a few steps. She clucked and snapped the reins, and he took one more step. "Buzz, please," she begged. "C'mon, boy, just turn around, and I promise we'll stop soon."

The stranger stepped outside and approached her horse. "Give me your whip. I'll get him moving for you."

"That won't be necessary, but thank you." Marva snapped the reins harder and tried to cluck, but her mouth had suddenly gone dry. "Buzz, walk on."

Buzz took one more step, champing at his bit and showing the whites of his eyes. The chained dog continued to bark, lunging and snarling and clawing at the ground with its front paws. Its owner ignored the clamor.

The strange man took hold of Buzz's bridle and led the horse around to face the track. But instead of letting go, he held on and appraised Marva with red-rimmed eyes. Grime streaked his throat, and the stench of him hung in the air.

"Your horse is tired. Why not step down and set a spell? You look like you could use a drink."

"Oh no, I'm expected at the lodge." Not at the Northwoods Oasis, but certainly she was expected back at Lakeland Lodge, so it wasn't a complete fabrication.

He smiled, showing blackened stumps of teeth. Approaching the cart, he took hold of the reins just in front of Marva's hand and jerked them from her grasp. His hand, easily the size of a baseball mitt, closed over her elbow. "Come on. I'll help you down."

Incoherent prayers flashed through Marva's mind as a wave of dizziness struck her.

Thudding hoofbeats approached on the track, and a rider

came into Marva's view. "Monte!" she whispered.

The stranger turned around at the approach of his new visitor, releasing his grasp on Marva's arm.

Monte trotted up on his bay mare. "Here you are. We were about to send out a search party, Miss Obermeier." He gave her a smile and a wink. "Sorry about the intrusion, Blanchard. This young lady has a talent for heading off on rabbit trails."

"Why are you out this way?" Blanchard growled.

"Following my guest, here. May we water our horses before we move on?"

Blanchard gave a sniff. "Help yourself." He lumbered back toward the house.

Monte dismounted, pumped fresh water into an algae-filled trough beside a broken hitching rail, and let both horses drink sparingly. "Take it slow, Buzz ol' boy." The horse rubbed his sweaty ears on Monte's shoulder. Marva watched them from her seat with a strange sense of detachment. She kept seeing black spots that wouldn't blink away.

Taking hold of Buzz's bridle, Monte led both horses along the track until they were out of sight of Blanchard's cabin. Then he led his mare to the back of the dogcart and tied her to a metal ring on the tailgate. Standing beside the cart, he handed Marva a canteen. "Scoot over. I'll drive."

Marva made room for him on the seat and handed over the reins. Relief flowed through her, and she took a long, shuddering breath. The black spots nearly filled her vision, and her head swam.

"Are you sure you still want to visit the Northwoods Oasis? Not to be unkind, but your face is red as a beet, and you look about ready to drop."

Great sobs suddenly shook her, and the canteen slipped from her limp fingers. Everything seemed confused after that.

nine

Therefore shall a man leave his father and his mother,
and shall cleave unto his wife: and they shall be one flesh.
GENESIS 2:24

"Miss Obermeier? Marva!" Monte caught the canteen, then grabbed Marva's arm before she could fall out of the dogcart. But she flopped forward and would have smashed her face on the dashboard if he hadn't caught her. "Marva!" Clutching her with both hands, he glanced around, trying to decide on his next move.

"Stand, Buzz," he told the horse. Holding Marva on the seat, Monte climbed down, then hefted her into his arms. She moaned softly and lifted one hand to her face.

He laid her on a bed of pine needles beneath a tree and removed her hat, then shrugged out of his coat and made it into a pad for her head. Next thing was to cool her off. He opened his canteen, lifted her head, and held the bottle to her dry lips. She drank a little, coughed, and tried to sit up. "No, just lie still. See if you can drink a few more swallows."

After taking another sip, she squinted up at him, her brow furrowed. "I feel awful."

"I think you've had too much sun. Just a minute." Pulling his handkerchief from his vest pocket, he hurried down to the lakeshore. He dunked the cloth and wrung it out, then returned to Marva's side.

Her eyes flew open when he laid the folded handkerchief on

her forehead. Instead of leaving it there, he patted it over her cheeks and temples. "That's nice. Thank you," she murmured, her eyes drifting shut again.

He took the opportunity to study her attire. A high-necked white shirtwaist and a skirt of some stiff, shiny blue fabric flattered her coloring and figure. However, such a trim and immobile waistline suggested stays, which would also explain her rapid, shallow breathing. But a gentleman could hardly suggest that she loosen her undergarments. "You might unbutton your collar," he suggested.

She gave him a shocked stare.

"I could toss you in the lake instead, I suppose. I've tried that method of cooling off, and I know it works." He grinned, and her lips twitched in response.

"Very well." When she reached for her collar, Monte turned away and loosened his own tie. He felt much better himself without that wool coat.

Picking his way back down to the lake's edge, he dipped his handkerchief in the water again to freshen it. "You'd best relax and rest here awhile longer. Then I think I'll take you to the Oasis and send for a doctor. We're not heading back to Lakeland Lodge until late afternoon. No more sun for you today, my lady."

She blinked up at him as he approached. Her flushed face made her eyes seem bluer than ever. "How did you come to be here?"

"I followed you," he admitted and knelt beside her. "Had to make sure you came to no harm. These Northwoods are not as domesticated as people like to think. Too many uncivilized loggers and drifters in the area."

"Mr. Stowell told you?"

"Told me that the map was for you? I already knew you

wanted to visit other lodges, so guessing didn't require great powers of deduction. I'm also guessing that you didn't request my escort for the day because your parents would disapprove." Monte talked while smoothing Marva's damp hair away from her face with his handkerchief. "What did they think of your taking this jaunt alone?"

She closed her eyes. "I didn't tell them."

"I see." He studied her tightly closed mouth and the flare of her nostrils. Aside from a few faint lines at the corners of her eyes and mouth, her skin was still nearly flawless. Even while damp and sweaty, her hair was fascinating. Such a handsome woman was seldom seen on the streets of Woodruff; he could scarcely blame other men for staring. Good women were still rare in these parts.

He slowly stroked the handkerchief down her cheek, letting his thumb slide over her skin. She gave a little gasp and held her breath. Her lashes fluttered, though her eyes remained shut. The wild thought struck him that he would like to kiss her. Startled, he scooted around to sit with his back against the pine's trunk, squeezing the handkerchief in his tight fist. The lake's color and sparkle resembled Marva's eyes.

A laugh rose in his throat, but he turned it into a cough. Obviously he had not been writing enough fiction lately, since his cowboy hero's poetic musings were starting to replace his own rational thoughts. Marva had made it clear way back in her first letter that she desired a marriage conducted like a mutually beneficial business partnership. *I neither expect nor desire romantic overtures.* She meant during courtship, surely. Or did she?

Tugging at his collar as if it choked him, he gave her a quick sideward glance and shook his head. Unless she married a man already on his deathbed, a platonic marriage would never work. And it *shouldn't* work. God had not ordained marriage to be a platonic relationship. From Monte's observations of Marva, admittedly limited, he suspected she wanted more from a marriage than her letters indicated, whether she realized it or not.

He would allow her to rest and recover for a few more minutes. They would have to return to the main road whether he took her to the lodge or back into Woodruff, and he wasn't eager to expose her to more afternoon sun.

"I hope that awful man doesn't come this way or release his dog," she said into a long silence. "I can't tell you how relieved I was to see you. I felt as if I might faint both from heat and from fear, and then what might have happened? God sent you. I know He did."

Monte couldn't honestly say that Blanchard would not have harmed her. "I know little about him, actually. Blanchard, I mean." He laced his hands around one upraised knee and pondered how to phrase his next statement. "I don't blame you for wanting a few hours to yourself, for wanting some privacy and independence, but it's just not safe for a woman to drive out alone around here."

Now would be the time to indicate that he knew why she wanted to interview local lodge owners, but he couldn't find the words. Come to think of it, why didn't she connect *him* with Lucky in Lakeland? He obviously fit the role. Her attitude was confusing, almost as if she hoped anyone besides Monte would prove to be her correspondent. It was slightly insulting, if he were entirely honest with himself.

She rolled to her side and sat up, leaning on one hand and rubbing her temple with the other. "I'm no longer overheated, but my head aches terribly." A thick lock of hair studded with two hairpins dipped over her shoulder.

"Drink more water." He shifted closer to her and held out the canteen.

She scooted over a little and accepted it, and for a moment, their eyes met. Tipping back her head, she drank. A little water dribbled down her chin and dripped on her blouse. She lowered the canteen and wiped the back of her hand over her lips. "Thank you."

He took it back and drank a few swallows himself. Anything to keep occupied. While screwing the lid back on, he considered his next move. "I want you to see a doctor. Sunstroke can be dangerous."

"I don't think I'm that ill. Mostly I just want to lie down in a cool, dark room and sleep. I feel. . .weak." Tears suddenly brimmed in her eyes. "And stupid."

"You're not stupid. Far from it." The tears were his undoing. He scooted just a little closer and put his arm around her shoulders, hoping she might see it as a fatherly move and allow the familiarity this once. His actual motivation was anything but paternal. To his surprise and delight, she laid her head on his chest and let her shoulder touch his side.

An unfamiliar blend of passion and protective tenderness whipped through his veins, making him feel twenty years younger. He rubbed her arm and tightened his grip, realizing in a flash that he was unprepared to handle this onslaught of temptation. A quick plea for strength gave him just enough willpower to sit upright and try to brush the moment aside. "We'd better get to the Oasis quickly. You can interview Hendricks while we wait for the doctor, if you feel well enough, that is."

❧

Marva sat upright. Monte's abrupt withdrawal stung her pride. She had sought only consolation and a safe haven. Did he imagine she'd been craving romance? Utterly ludicrous! Tears burned her cheeks until she wiped them away.

He brushed off his trousers and offered her a hand up. She thought about ignoring his offer but reconsidered. Her head still swam, and she still felt sick. After shifting to a position from which she could rise, she gripped his hand. It felt warm and rough with calluses.

He pulled her up, but her legs refused to cooperate. Again he caught her before she could pitch forward on her face, quickly shifting his grip to her shoulders. The world spun around her, and her stomach roiled.

"Marva, can you walk, or should I carry you?"

"I can walk," she tried to say, but it came out sounding more like a breathy wail ending in a sob.

He put one arm behind her shoulders and the other behind her knees and scooped her off the ground. She felt him stagger to regain his balance, but otherwise he didn't seem overly strained by her weight. Wrapping her arms around his neck, she hid her face in his shoulder and tried to pretend he was someone else. Anyone else.

He gently deposited her on the seat of the dogcart, waited to make sure she could sit upright unattended, and then went back to retrieve her hat and his coat. Marva's vision narrowed to a small tunnel of reality; everything else was black. Yet when she closed her eyes, she was fully aware of her surroundings. She felt the cart tip to one side when Monte climbed in beside her; she felt his shoulder bump hers, then the comforting warmth of his arm sliding around her and pressing her toward him. She heard him exhale a deep breath just above her head. Her position was awkward, yet she knew it enabled him both to drive and to make sure she didn't fall out of the cart.

Monte shook the reins and clucked. Marva heard the creak

of harness and the clop of Buzz's hooves, and the cart lurched forward. Light flickered over her eyelids, and motion freshened the air on her face. She drew a deep, shaky breath and let it out in a sigh.

How would he treat her during the remaining days of her vacation at the lodge? She couldn't help but wonder why he had chosen to follow her. What if Harding Stowell had come to her rescue? How very different she would feel about resting against *his* shoulder! Monte Van Huysen was easily the most attractive man of her acquaintance, married or single. Why couldn't he have been her newspaper correspondent?

If she had waited for God's timing and not attempted to find herself a husband, she would have met Monte without her head full of plots to hunt down a certain lodge owner, and maybe, just maybe, something might have developed between them. It might still. After all, he might come to Longtree to visit his brother's family sometime. And if he did, she might encounter him at church or in town. . . .

Marva had little experience interpreting the behavior of men, and though she was probably ridiculously mistaken, her heart conceived the tiniest hope that Monte found her attractive. Not in her current sunburned, bedraggled condition, of course, but maybe at her best, she might catch his eye. Just maybe. Any hope at all was better than none.

If only her head would stop spinning.

ten

Wherefore be ye not unwise,
but understanding what the will of the Lord is.
EPHESIANS 5:17

The sun had dropped behind the tallest trees before Marva succeeded in convincing Mel Hendricks, owner of the Northwoods Oasis, that she felt well enough for Monte to drive her home that evening. Monte wrapped his arm around her shoulders with a proprietary air as he escorted her out to the waiting dogcart.

Seeing his rifle on the floorboards as she climbed to her seat, Marva looked up at him, wide-eyed.

He climbed in beside her. "Just in case. I don't expect trouble, but it's best to be prepared."

After a quick wave at Hendricks, he clucked up Buzz and headed home. Petunia, tied to the cart, trotted behind.

Although dark circles underlined her eyes, Marva sat upright on the seat beside Monte, chin up, shoulders back, hands folded in her lap. She wore her jacket again now that the temperature had cooled, and he once again wore his sack coat, conforming to propriety.

"Mr. Hendricks was kind to send for the doctor, but it was unnecessary," she said into a peaceful silence. "I simply had too much sun."

"Better to be safe." He clucked Buzz into a faster jog. "I hope your parents aren't worried."

"I do, too."

A flock of ducks flew overhead, quacking, headed toward Johnson Lake.

"Did you have a chance to interview Mr. Hendricks?"

"No, but it doesn't matter. I've abandoned the idea."

"What idea?"

As he expected, she didn't answer the question.

"We should be home within the hour, before dark. The drive home should be faster than your drive out, since I don't reckon on taking the scenic route like you did. I lighted the side lamps just in case we don't beat the dark, but we shouldn't need them."

"I'm not very good with maps." Her voice sounded humble. "You also carry the gun 'just in case.' What kind of 'trouble' might we encounter?"

He rolled his shoulders and heard his spine crackle. He gave her a quick glance, hoping she hadn't noticed. "Oh, maybe a bear. Maybe a drunken drifter. You never know in these parts. The rifle wouldn't do us much good if I left it in the scabbard on Petunia's saddle."

"Have you shot a bear before?"

"Sure. Out in Wyoming, that was. Nothing but blackies around here, but we used to shoot grizzlies out West. Big, mean bears."

"Myles got attacked by a grizzly bear back home."

"Huh, not in southern Wisconsin, he didn't. He must have been pulling your leg."

"No, it was a grizzly bear. It escaped from a circus."

Monte thought about that one. "If you say so."

She chuckled. "You don't believe me."

"I didn't say that."

"You didn't have to say it. Ask Myles when we get home. He'll tell you. It stole a steer from Obadiah Watson—he's Beulah's stepfather—and when the men hunted it down, it nearly killed Myles. That was right around the time he committed his life to God."

"Really? He didn't tell me that story. I'll have to pound it out of him."

"Spoken like a true big brother."

He smiled at her, then couldn't look away.

"What?" she inquired, looking self-conscious yet pleased.

"Smile again."

She smiled readily but covered her cheek with one hand. He pulled her hand down.

"You have a dimple in your right cheek. I noticed before but didn't really notice."

She turned her face away.

"Why have you never married, Marva? You're a lovely woman, sweet, able—I don't understand it."

She touched her cheek again but kept her face averted. "The right man never came along. I waited patiently for God's timing, but it never happened."

He recognized sadness and a hint of bitterness in her voice. "You could still marry now." Realizing how that comment might be construed, he faced forward and studied Buzz's hindquarters. The horse had dropped to a walk without his noticing.

"The right man would have to ask." Her voice trembled as if with restrained tears. "I spent years being angry with God because He never gave me the husband I wanted. All those years gone, wasted! I should have enjoyed each day as it came and recognized that if I remained single it was because God knew singleness was best for me."

Had she married years ago, she would likely not be available to marry Monte now. This fact occurred to him while she spoke. But should he be so arrogant as to imagine that God had reserved such a woman and set her aside to be his bride?

"Why have you never married?" She returned the question.

"I've never asked a woman to marry me."

"But why not? Surely you have met many attractive women during your travels." Although she spoke lightly, he sensed heaviness underlying the questions.

"None that I wanted to share my life with."

She turned on the seat and fixed him with a quizzical stare from beneath her hat's brim. "But why ever not? Are you so difficult to please? Or do you conceal some dark secret in your past?"

That last question struck home. She obviously did not know—Beulah must not have told her—or she would never have spoken so lightly.

"I never stay in one place long enough to suit a woman," he improvised. "Some men aren't cut out for marriage."

"But you—" She fell silent.

"But I what?"

"Never mind."

A mosquito whined in Monte's ear. He smacked himself on the side of the head and knocked his hat askew. "Bugs are bad tonight."

"They seem to be bad most every night."

The first stars glimmered in the steel gray sky above. "It won't be long now. I hope they saved us some supper."

"I'm not hungry, but for your sake, I hope so, too."

Before he turned off the main road into his long driveway, the last glimmers of twilight had faded and stars filled the night sky. The bobbing lanterns threw small puddles of light that scarcely reached the nearest trees. One of the dogcart's wheels bumped into a pothole, and Marva bumped into Monte's shoulder. "Sorry about that," he said teasingly.

"I shall try to forgive you," she retorted calmly.

He grinned, and a sudden wave of affection for her rolled over him. Driving along with this woman at his side felt right somehow. He could easily imagine spending the rest of his life in her company, and the thought started a longing ache in his soul.

As they approached the lodge grounds, a bonfire's glow appeared between the trees. Hardy must have lighted it for the guests, who sat on the log benches around the fire pit, singing hymns. He slowed his horse, thinking Marva might like to join her companions, but she laid her hand on his forearm. "Please don't stop. I need to go to my room."

Without a word, he drove the dogcart to the lodge steps, secured the reins, and came around to help Marva alight.

Lanterns burned dimly on either side of the main door. No one sat on the porch tonight; the lodgers must all be down by the bonfire. Marva reached out to take his hand. Her grip felt uncertain. Courage and determination must be keeping her upright. He sensed that she was ready to collapse. Releasing her hand, he reached for her waist to lift her down. She murmured a token protest. He set her on her feet, facing him, but did not let go. "Can you walk?"

Her head bobbed. "I think so."

"I don't." For the third time that day, he hefted her into his arms then mounted the porch steps and fumbled for the latch. She simply let her head bob against his shoulder.

Once inside, he carried her across the foyer. No one was behind the desk. He entered the hall, trying to avoid bashing her head or feet on anything, then walked its length and stopped at the door to her room. It was unlocked, so he pushed it open and carried her inside. Guessing which bed was hers, he laid her on it. "Marva, are you all right?" he said, trying to stop gasping for breath. His heart raced, mostly from exertion.

"I'm. . .terribly. . .sleepy," she mumbled as if drugged.

He untied her hat and tugged it off her head. Her forehead was warm but not feverish. He gripped her hand and considered what to do next. Feeling around at the foot of the bed, he located a wool blanket, which he spread over her. He would have liked to remove her shoes, but that seemed too personal.

"I'll let you rest now," he said, reluctant to leave her alone. Deep, steady breathing was her only reply. He smiled. Once more he touched her forehead then bent way over and kissed her soft cheek. "Good night, my dear."

❧

"Marva! Marva. . .why, you slept in your clothes! Whatever possessed you to do that? Where were you all day yesterday? Your father and I began to worry when you didn't show up at the bonfire."

They hadn't worried until then? Marva sighed and reached up to push tickling hair from her face. She groaned. Every muscle ached, and her head still felt heavy.

"I went for a drive and got lost. Mr. Van Huysen found me and drove me back home. I had too much sun." She shifted her legs over the side of the bed and watched listlessly as the blanket slithered to the floor.

"You'll have to repeat that, since not one word of it was clear." Mother sounded irritable. Mother was never irritable.

Marva straightened her shoulders and groaned again. "I hurt everywhere."

"Now that I understood."

Mother stood beside the bed in her faded lavender dressing gown, her silver braid hanging over one shoulder. Her normally serene face was creased with frown lines.

Slowly Marva repeated her explanation, holding out her blistered hands for her mother's inspection.

"I should say you did have too much sun! Child, will you never develop good sense? Why did you drive out alone, and without gloves, and on such a hot day? We can be grateful that Mr. Van Huysen found you, or you might have become hopelessly lost in these dreadful woods!" She suddenly clasped Marva in a tight hug. "The Lord watched over you, for certain. Had I known all this before I went to bed last night, I'm sure I wouldn't have slept a wink! We saw you sleeping when we came in after the bonfire last night, but I never dreamed. . ."

"I'm fine, Mother, only rather tired and blistered."

"Marva, is there anything you want to tell—"

A knock at the door brought her mother upright in an instant. "Now who could that be? Your papa went fishing." She hurried to remove the chain lock.

"Ma'am." Marva heard a woman's voice say. "Miss Obermeier's bath is ready in the washroom across the hall. We left extra rinse water."

Mother paused then said, "Thank you very much. I'll tell her." Closing the door, she regarded her daughter in surprise. "You ordered a bath?"

Marva blinked in confusion. "There must be some mistake."

Her mother's head tilted. "Actually, you could use one. Why not take it, since it's already prepared for you?"

Reaching one hand up to her hair, which was stiff with sweat and road dust, Marva nodded. A bath sounded like heaven.

Minutes later, she soaked in steaming, rose-scented water in a huge aluminum tub. Her hair floated around her shoulders. Her sunburned hands stung in the water, but her aching muscles began to relax.

She remembered Monte carrying her into the lodge the night before. Or at least she had vague but lovely memories of his comforting arms and gentle voice, the scratchiness of his coat against her cheek, the bump of her foot against a doorpost, and his apology. He had laid her on the bed. She knew that much but recalled nothing afterward.

Tightness built in her throat. He was so dear! So kind and considerate and gentlemanly! Why had such a man never come into her life before now?

Hot tears blended with the water while she rinsed soap from her hair. Yet a faint hope grew within her that maybe, just maybe, *now* was God's perfect timing.

eleven

Every way of a man is right in his own eyes:
but the LORD *pondereth the hearts.*
PROVERBS 21:2

"Watch me, Ma!"

Jerry Van Huysen jumped off the swim platform with a modest splash. When he surfaced, Beulah and Marva applauded and exclaimed to the boy's satisfaction. Myles treaded water nearby, watching over the flock of young swimmers.

Listening with one ear to Beulah's chatter, Marva tried to soak in the beauty of her surroundings, to store it up for memories. This picnic was the last event of the Longtree vacationers' holiday at the lodge. Tomorrow they would load back on the train and head south. Somewhere behind her she heard Monte's deep chuckle. He must be talking with one of the other families. Would he come and sit with his brother's family to eat his meal?

An ache rose inside her chest. The idea of leaving, of never seeing this beautiful place again—of never seeing Monte again—did not bear contemplation.

"Funniest story you ever heard. . ." he was saying. His voicc faded for several beats, then she heard ". . .still doesn't know the truth." Laughter followed.

Hearing Beulah speak Monte's name, Marva refocused on the current conversation. ". . .come back anytime we want to. You know, he insisted that we pay nothing for our lodging, but of course it would be best if that news didn't spread since he and Mr. Stowell can hardly afford to lodge our entire group for free."

"He and Mr. Stowell?"

Beulah spooned applesauce into Ginny's waiting mouth. "Yes. They're partners, you know. Mr. Stowell bought half ownership of the lodge last winter. He runs most of the business end of things. That way Monte has time for his writing again. I thought you knew all this."

Marva tried not to let her face reveal her confusion. "I probably heard it at one time but forgot. You're saying that Lakeland Lodge originally belonged entirely to your husband's brother? He owns the lodge?"

Beulah nodded. "Monte's been keeping track of our family for years, mostly by reading our town newspaper. He got the idea of advertising his lodge in the *Longtree Enquirer,* and of course it worked. We came without any idea that Myles's brother lived here. All our arrangements were made through Mr. Stowell."

"Oh." Without any idea—she could relate to that part.

"I thought you knew all this, Marva," Beulah said again. "You were at our house that first night when Monte explained everything."

"I must have been outside with Trixie during that part of the story." Marva's heart pounded so hard that she felt dizzy. All this time she had assumed Monte merely worked at the lodge as fishing and hunting guide. Remembering his air of command, his office inside the lodge, and the respect shown him by staff members, she suddenly felt stupid. How blind could a woman be?

She rested her forehead on her open hand. "But why the secrecy? Why didn't he come to Longtree to visit his brother? I don't understand."

Beulah sat up straight, a spoonful of applesauce poised in midair. "If you didn't hear him tell his story, I really don't think it's my place to pass it on to you. He had his reasons, Marva. Maybe you should ask him yourself."

Ginny voiced a protest, and the applesauce quickly entered her mouth.

Marva tried to laugh, but it sounded strangled. "I hardly know him well enough for that, Beulah. You're right—it's not my business to know his motivations."

A step sounded behind her, and Monte himself settled beside Marva on the quilt, folding his long legs awkwardly. "Hello, ladies. I hope you're enjoying this fine day. I ordered it for your pleasure."

"So thoughtful of you, brother," Beulah said with a smile. "I also appreciate your getting the applesauce for Ginny. She was too hungry to wait."

Ginny crawled across the quilt and climbed into her uncle's lap, smiling from ear to ear. Monte appeared startled yet pleased.

"Oh, let me clean her up," Marva offered. "She'll get apple-sauce all over you."

The baby protested, but Monte held her still so Marva could wipe her chubby face.

"Thank you." His eyes twinkled. "I hope you're all as hungry as Ginny. The kitchen crew prepared a feast. They'll be setting up on the outdoor tables soon."

"My tribe is working up an appetite." Beulah indicated Myles and the swimming boys. "Some of the men are fishing—their last opportunity to catch that monster fish."

"My father never caught a muskie, but he can't say enough about his half-dozen nice walleye and that big bass he pulled in last week," Marva said.

"And Myles and the boys must have nearly emptied this side of the lake of bluegill and perch." Beulah chuckled. "Monte, this has been the most wonderful, relaxing holiday! We can never thank you enough."

He focused on Ginny, who had pulled out his tie to chew on. "Don't try. These have been some of the best days of my life, too."

Marva caught his glance in her direction. What, exactly, was he implying? A trickle of doubt entered her turbulent pool of thought. Was he playing a joke on her? Had he written notes under the name of "Lucky in Lakeland" to build up a lonely woman's dreams only as an amusing diversion?

Had he known all the time that her search for an unmarried lodge owner was actually a search for him? If so, and she began to suspect that this was the case, he had a cruel sense of humor and was not the man she had believed him to be.

He had attended the church meetings Rev. Schoengard held on Sundays and entered into the worship with apparent sincerity. Was it all an act?

Or had his letters been sincere? Beulah's intimation of some secret in Monte's past made her think. Hadn't Myles mentioned something years ago about his deceased brother's scandalous past? But she couldn't recall the details. Maybe Monte feared rejection. Could her own self-doubt and insecurity cause her to misjudge the intentions of a good man? How could she learn the truth?

"I invited some local acquaintances to the picnic," Monte said. "They should arrive soon. Two of the local vacation lodge owners. You'll remember Mr. Hendricks, Miss Obermeier. He is eager to see you again."

His sidelong glance held a glimmer of mischief, and Marva's suspicions strengthened. He was laughing at her!

Trixie suddenly tripped on the edge of the quilt and crash-landed beside Marva, bringing with her an abundance of sand. An instant later, a very wet and sand-encrusted hound vaulted the toddler and sprawled in the middle of the quilt, tail lashing.

"Ralph! Off," Monte shouted. "Bad dog."

By the time the quilt had been shaken out, sand brushed from the toddler, and the dog tied up at Monte's cabin, the lodge staff had finished setting out a picnic luncheon on tables in the open area near the playground. Myles took the boys up to their cabin to change out of their swimming costumes while Beulah and Marva prepared plates for them.

As the children distracted his relatives, Monte pulled Marva aside for a moment. "Would you like me to bring them to you here, or shall I introduce you later?"

"Of whom are you speaking?"

"Mr. Hendricks and Mr. DeSamprio."

"Why did you invite them here?" Anger sharpened her voice.

"To help you out, of course. I know you never got the chance to interview Hendricks the other day."

Hot blood rushed into her face. She could think of nothing, absolutely nothing, to say. Did he know? He must know! And if he knew, he *must* be. . . Anger and humiliation fomented in her belly until she felt ill. Rather than spew out questions and accusations, she jerked her arm from his grasp and returned to Beulah, who was, thankfully, too distracted by her children's disputes and scuffles to notice Marva's agitation.

❧

Monte had a sudden impulse to go beat his head against a tree. *Idiot!*

Startling revelations raced through his head. Rather than

think through his jumbled motivations, he hurried away to find Pete DeSamprio and Mel Hendricks, the two lodge owners he had invited to join the picnic. Their company might serve to distract him from guilty thoughts and convictions.

Neither of the visitors had any idea why he had invited them to join his lodge picnic, but they dug into the spread of food without reservation. "Good chow, Van Huysen," DeSamprio said, shifting a mouthful into one cheek. "Great view. You ask us here to rub our noses in it, or what?"

Monte tried to smile. "Maybe we can get tips and ideas from each other and band together to bring more business north. This group read about my lodge in their local newspaper. We offered reduced rates for a large party."

At that moment, the minister requested silence for a blessing on the food. DeSamprio and Hendricks followed Monte's lead by removing their hats and bowing their heads. Rev. Schoengard gave thanks for the luncheon, requesting God's blessing on those who had prepared it and asking for safety during tomorrow's journey home. As soon as the pastor said, "Amen," the men resumed eating.

Monte brightened, seeing Hardy strolling in their direction with a loaded plate in hand. He waved his partner over. "Join us." Within minutes, Hardy had the two men discussing advertising and profit margins, and Monte could let his attention wander.

Casually he scanned the grounds for Marva. To his surprise, she was seated at the next picnic table with her parents and the Schoengards. He rested his elbow on the tabletop and his chin on his palm and let his eyes drink her in. With her white skin and that stunning hair against the backdrop of the deep blue lake, she made a striking picture.

She glanced up and caught his gaze but immediately looked away. He watched her try but fail to finish her luncheon.

Folding her napkin, she laid it on her plate and glanced once more at Monte. He smiled and nodded. A little frown line appeared between her brows, and she quickly stood up.

Monte rose to intercept her as she left the table. "Leave your plate on the table. The staff will clean up."

She set down her plate. "Do you have something of importance to say, Mr. Van Huysen?"

"You don't wish to talk to Mr. DeSamprio and Mr. Hendricks?"

"I do not." She propped her fists on her hips and looked him in the eye. "If you have nothing further to say, I believe I shall go inside and begin packing."

"You look lovely today, Miss Obermeier. Like. . .like summertime."

She bobbed a curtsy. "Why, thank you, kind sir. Good day." And she walked away.

He winced behind her back.

Jealous of his own pseudonym, that's what he was. Why couldn't Marva forget her newspaper beau and love *him*—just plain Monte Van Huysen? Did she find him irritating in person? Maybe he smelled bad or had some annoying habit of which he was unaware.

Hardy approached him and clapped him on the shoulder. "I know just how you feel. That is one peculiar woman. I imagine she's mentioned to you a man who communicated with her through a newspaper."

"I know something about it."

Hardy chuckled without mirth. "I figured she asked you to invite Pete and Mel here. Did she ever talk to them?"

"No."

"Can't say I'm surprised. I'm thinking she's the type who likes a man in theory better than a man in the flesh. Try not to break your heart over her pretty face, partner. You won't be the first or the last, I'd guess. Oh look—there goes Mel after her."

Sure enough, Mel Hendricks followed Marva toward the lodge. Monte barely restrained a groan.

❧

Marva gritted her teeth to keep back tears. She had to force a smile at Dorothy Hilbert when she passed her on the path to the lodge; almost everyone else must be down at the shore. She could only hope her parents would linger and talk for at least another hour, giving her time to control her overwrought emotions.

That man! That beast! She wanted to kick him in the shins. She would love to give his mustache a sharp tug and smack the smile off his face. How dare he mock her openly! How dare he bring those men to meet her!

"Miss Obermeier!"

At the sound of this hail, she turned on the path. Mr. Hendricks approached, his smile revealing a gold tooth. "I trust you're fully recovered? Mr. Van Huysen told me the other day that you'd attempted to drive to my lodge to interview me. Do you write for a Milwaukee paper?"

"No sir, I don't." Heat rolled up Marva's throat and flooded her cheeks. "I simply wished to. . . Oh, never mind. The reason no longer exists. I'm ever so sorry you came all this way to no purpose."

Puzzlement spread over his pleasant face. "It was no trouble, I assure you. Mr. Stowell told me you especially wished to interview unmarried lodge owners in the Northwoods. I'm a widower. Does that count?"

She shook her head. "The man I'm looking for has never married. Thank you anyway, Mr. Hendricks."

She turned and rushed up the lodge steps before he could

say another word. Once inside, she ran to her empty room and started packing. Anger flowed through her every movement, and she had to refold several items before she could pack them.

I don't care if I ever see that man again!

Was he really a jokester without a sensible thought in his head? No, that was too harsh a judgment. Myles and Beulah esteemed him highly, and the children adored their uncle. He had befriended most of the men in the party while guiding them to the best fishing spots on the lake.

And Marva would never forget his gentle strength and thoughtfulness the day she went looking for Lucky and got lost. That day, he had been a true hero.

Marva was uncertain what her parents thought of him, beyond his abilities with the lodge.

Tired of packing, she sat on the side of her bed and let her thoughts drift. How smug he had looked at the picnic, staring openly at her with that silly smile on his face! Why did he have to be so handsome? It would be much easier to dislike him if she could only find him physically disgusting.

She bent over and pulled her packet of newspaper clippings from the drawer of her bedside table. Leafing through the few papers, she read over Lucky's words—Monte's words?—and wondered again if Monte Van Huysen concealed a sensitive, serious heart behind his charming manner.

❧

"You're not coming to supper?" Mother repeated with concern in her voice. "But it's our last night here, Marva. Everyone will miss you."

"I have a headache," Marva answered truthfully. "Please make my excuses, Mother. I'm truly not up to socializing this evening."

She felt her mother's cool hand on her forehead, then her cheeks. "Too much sun again, maybe. Is there anything you wish to tell me, dear one? I saw you talking with Mr. Van Huysen at the picnic, and then you disappeared. He seemed quieter than usual all afternoon."

"Don't read too much into that," Papa said. "A man can have many reasons for being thoughtful that have nothing to do with a woman, difficult though that may be for you to believe." He gave his wife a wink and squeezed her shoulder.

Mother looked chagrined. "I do tend to imagine too much at times, and I know my speculations have caused you hurt in the past, Marva dear."

Marva knew her mother referred not only to the long-ago misunderstanding with Myles, but also to imaginary interest from dozens of other eligible men over the years. She reached up to take her mother's hand. "It's not your fault. I do the same thing—read too much into people's emotional states and assume they all relate somehow to me." Hearing a betraying quiver in her voice, she smiled and fell silent.

Her mother's eyes held sympathetic understanding. "Tomorrow will be a long day. You just rest. I'll see if we can't bring you a little something to eat."

twelve

Now the God of hope fill you with all joy and peace in believing, that ye may abound in hope, through the power of the Holy Ghost.
ROMANS 15:13

Marva busied herself with arranging her bags in the overhead compartments, trying not to eavesdrop on the farewells between Monte and his relatives, yet at the same time straining to catch each word he spoke. Would he take time to bid her an individual farewell? There would be no privacy in this crowded train car, and she had no reason to return to the platform. . . not that privacy could be found there either.

Her hatbox kept popping out of position and threatening to drop on the head of the passenger seated beneath it, who happened to be Caroline Schoengard, the minister's wife. "Excuse me—I'm so sorry—" Marva reached over the other woman's head one more time to shove the box back in place. Caroline claimed not to mind, but Marva sensed her irritation. Everyone was tired and edgy, dreading the long train ride home.

"Here, let me." Monte reached around Marva to rearrange the boxes. Grateful and shaking in every limb, she stood back to watch. "There. That should stay put." He lowered his arms.

"Thank you."

"Yes, thank you," Mrs. Schoengard added. "Now I don't have to worry about something dropping on my head at any moment."

Monte smiled briefly at her, then focused on Marva. "Was that your last box?"

She nodded.

"Where are you sitting?"

She pointed to the row. "With my parents, for now."

"Until Beulah needs you," he added.

The train blasted a long whistle. People raised their voices above the clamor. The cacophony bombarded Marva's ears, and fear blocked her throat. Desperately she wanted to ask the question—this might be her last opportunity ever!—but how could she ask it amid all this confusion?

Someone bumped into her from behind. Monte quickly placed his hand on the small of her back in a protective gesture. A party of strangers had entered at the front of the car and appeared determined to make their way to the rear, shuffling everyone in the aisle aside or ahead. A carpetbag struck Marva between the shoulder blades; angry voices protested on all sides.

Monte guided her to the back of the train carriage. A lady climbed the steps and pushed past them. This time Monte bracketed Marva with his arms, protecting her from wayward luggage. He looked down into her face, shook his head, and smiled briefly. "I don't believe we're going to find a more private place than this to say our good-byes. I hope you'll forgive me for staring at you yesterday. It was rude, I know."

"Certainly," she said, brushing that awkward request aside, "and thank you for a lovely vacation, Mr. Van Huysen. You did so much for my parents and for all our friends. I imagine you'll be visiting your brother and his family sometime." Formality was difficult to maintain while he stood so close.

He suddenly gripped her hand and looked down at it, then up into her eyes, and then down at her hand again. His fingers pressed hers, his thumb rumpled her glove, and then he took a step back without meeting her gaze and breathed as if he'd sprinted to catch the train.

Marva waited, expecting him to make some declaration or comment. He seemed to be deadly earnest. In fact, he behaved almost like a man in love. . .but then, how would she know how a man in love behaves? Actually, he looked more like a man in pain.

"Mr. Van Huysen, are you well?"

The conductor bellowed his last boarding call. Monte jerked as if he'd been struck. "I—I'll be visiting sometime. Like you said." He squeezed his eyes shut and heaved a sigh. "Thank you. Meeting you was—I hope we meet again. Sometime. I—" The train gave a lurch, and his eyes popped wide.

"Marva."

"Yes?"

"Good-bye." He released her hand, bolted down the steps, and disappeared.

Marva caught herself as the train gave another jolt and straining metal screamed in protest. Using the seat backs for leverage, she staggered up the aisle and slipped into the vacant seat beside her mother.

"Mr. Van Huysen is waving to us from the platform, Marva. You should wave at him." Her mother sounded pleased. "I do hope he comes to visit Myles and Beulah. I hope you don't mind my saying this, but I think he admired you, dear."

Marva caught a glimpse of Monte and Hardy Stowell standing side by side, waving. Monte held his hat over his heart with a funereal air. Pulling a handkerchief from her pocketbook, she waved it at him. As the train gained momentum, the buildings along Front Street slipped out of view; as the train cars moved onto the trestle, the clacking changed in tone.

Would she ever see this little town again? Sparkling sunlight on the lake's brilliant blue surface brought tears to her eyes. Was that a loon's white breast in the distance? An open window brought a whiff of water and pine. The breeze felt cool against her damp cheeks. Why was she crying?

She lowered her handkerchief and wiped her eyes and nose. Depression weighted her chest like a stone. How she longed for privacy, the chance to release her emotions in a storm of tears!

"Marva?"

She looked up. Myles wore an apologetic expression. "Beulah is hoping you'll help us with the children. Trixie is nearly frantic, and the baby needs to be fed."

She nodded and rose. It was good to be needed.

❧

Monte watched the train cars slip past. Once he took a step forward, determined to catch hold and climb aboard one of the passing coaches. It wasn't too late! He could still grab on. . . .

The last car rattled past, and the train slid over the trestle, its noise gradually fading in the distance. He found himself breathing in deep gasps. Why? Why hadn't he told her? The words were simple enough: "I am Lucky in Lakeland. I love you. Please marry me."

But no, it wasn't that simple. Marriage involved much, much more.

He would see her again. Myles had demanded a visit from him before the end of the year. This wasn't his last chance. He could work up a plan, a perfect way to propose marriage and sweep her off her feet. Heavenly visions of a future with Marva drifted through his imagination.

But between him and that idyllic future loomed his past.

It would be so much easier to pretend he had never met Marva Obermeier and simply resume his undemanding bachelor lifestyle. With luck, he could avoid mentioning his unsavory past to anyone ever again. It was nobody's business anyway. He'd made no promises; Marva would expect nothing from him. If Lucky in Lakeland never placed another ad in the paper, she might be disappointed, but she would soon forget and move on with her life. A woman that wonderful wouldn't remain single forever. It was nothing short of a miracle that she had remained unmarried this long.

"Monte, are you gonna stand here all day?"

He turned to stare at Hardy's sweaty pink face. "No."

His voice sounded so weak that Hardy's brows lifted in evident surprise.

Monte pulled himself together and said more firmly, "No. Just admiring the view."

"Really? Whatever you say."

He followed Hardy's glance toward the train yard, weedy, grimy, and strewed with refuse. "No, the lake." He waved his arm. "Out there. It's a gorgeous day. Blue sky, blue lake."

His partner's lopsided smile told Monte he was getting nowhere. "You head back, Hardy. I've got to stop for mail and supplies."

"Right." Hardy gave him an ironical salute and walked away, shaking his head.

Monte could ignore the heaviness in his spirit as long as he kept working, but the long, solitary drive home allowed far too much thinking time. Propping his elbows on his knees, he bowed his head over the reins clutched in his hands. Shoulders hunched, he let the regret flood over him.

"Coward," he muttered. Then louder, "Coward!"

Buzz and Petunia flicked their ears back as if to listen and tossed their heads in seeming uncertainty. "Do you hear?" he said in a calmer tone. "Your master is an idiot and a coward."

He tipped his head back and sighed deeply. "I did it again, God. When will I learn?" Tension stabbed at his temples and tightened his shoulders. "I'm still afraid. What if she rejects me when she knows?" The perfect weather seemed to mock his misery. How could skies be blue while storms raged in his heart?

For over twenty years, he had carried around the wreckage caused by sin. Sure, God had forgiven him—his eternity in heaven was guaranteed through Christ's cleansing blood. But here on earth, he still dragged a burden of guilt behind him wherever he went.

"Why, God? I want to be free!"

Trust Me.

The words came into his head, not as a voice but as a clear message.

Blinking, he looked up as if expecting to see God in the sky.

❧

That evening Monte still wrestled with his questions and argued with God's clear request. After tossing on his bed for hours, he finally lit a lamp and opened his Bible. Turning to the place marked by a ribbon, the passage in Matthew where he had left off reading that morning, he glared at the page. "If You have something to tell me, I'm looking. I've got to have peace, God. If You don't give it to me, I don't know where to turn."

This disrespectful prayer was the best he could manage at the moment. Hopefully God would bear with him. At least he was turning to the Bible instead of a bottle.

He let his tired eyes drift down the page. Chapter 7. Jesus

was talking about beams and hypocrites. Pearls and swine. He sniffed and, with one finger, rubbed his mustache.

Then verse 7 caught his attention. " 'Ask, and it shall be given you. . . .' " He read through the section. " 'Or what man is there of you, whom if his son ask bread, will he give him a stone? . . . If ye then, being evil, know how to give good gifts unto your children, how much more shall your Father which is in heaven give good things to them that ask him?' "

Monte sat up, swung his legs over the side of his bed, and rested his forehead on his clenched fists. "But God, if I ask for Marva, what if You say, 'No'? Surely You don't mean that I'm supposed to ask for something specific, just for my own pleasure. Do You?"

No matter how he might beat around the bush when he prayed, requesting peace, asking for love, begging for a wife, one obvious fact remained: Both he and God knew that Marva and none other was on his mind. He might as well be honest.

"Dear God." He paused and then amended, "Dear Lord God, You know my heart's desire. You know I want Marva Obermeier as my wife. Please, Lord, I want her to love me! I know You don't force people to love each other, but I don't know how else to ask this. I'm a miserable beast and entirely unworthy of a woman like her. I feel like an idiot for even asking this. . .but You tell me over and over again to trust You, so I'm trying my best."

thirteen

Thou wilt keep him in perfect peace,
whose mind is stayed on thee: because he trusteth in thee.
Isaiah 26:3

Marva put one hand to the small of her back and rubbed, leaning on the top rail of the pigpen. The pigs snorted and squabbled over their slop, ears flopping, snouts wriggling. The shoats had grown and fattened nicely over the summer and would provide some good eating over winter. Papa intended to sell several of them, but others would soon hang in pieces in the smokehouse.

J. D. Parker, the hired man, sauntered past her and tipped his hat. Marva merely nodded. Although she usually appreciated good manners, his behavior—or maybe it was his expression—seemed too familiar for their degree of acquaintance.

The hog stench finally got to be too much. She entered the barn and climbed the ladder to the hayloft—her first time up there in many years. The rich hay aroma, the golden motes of dust revealed by sunlight slipping through cracks in the barn walls, and the mounds of hay stored for winter feed all created a sense of nostalgia, of slipping back through time. Seating herself near the loft door, her back against a prickly wall of hay, she gazed out across the Wisconsin countryside and felt like a child again. A lonely, listless child in a middle-aged woman's body.

Late summer sunshine flowed over the fields of corn and

wheat. A breeze made ripples across the expanse like waves on a huge, golden lake. Her mind instantly pictured a sun-flecked blue surface with reflections of silver-birch trunks against the dark, upside-down images of pines. She heard again the slap of water against the shore and the quacking of ducks. The wind against her face brought back the sigh of pines and the rustle of oak and maple leaves instead of cornstalks.

This ache in her soul—how could she bear it?

"Marva?" her father called from below.

She was tempted to remain quiet and preserve her peace. "In the loft, Papa." She heard his boots on the ladder rungs.

"What are you doing up here?" His head rose through the trapdoor, bits of hay dangling from hair and beard.

"Nothing much."

"Your mother's been looking for you." He rested his forearms on the loft floor, still standing on the ladder. "I've been meaning to tell you that I'm gonna hire J. D. Parker on full time. He kept the place up well while we were away last month, and I like the way he tends to things as if this place were his own. I disapprove of the way he frequents local taverns, but since the drink doesn't interfere with his work, I can't complain."

Marva nodded. "I'm sorry I can't help you more."

He snorted. "A farm needs a man to work it. You've done more'n your share around this place since you were a little thing. It's time to face facts. I'm too old to keep it up."

Gazing at her father's weathered face and stooping shoulders, Marva knew he was right. "Are you planning to sell the farm?"

He climbed all the way up, brushed off his trousers, and then sat beside her and chewed on a straw. "I'd always thought to hand it on to you, once you married, but I don't see that plan coming about unless you suddenly take a shine to Parker." He gave her a teasing wink. "I know you love the place, but your heart isn't fastened to it. To be honest, I ain't so dead set on living out my days here as I used to be."

Marva pondered this in silence, doubting his words. Papa's roots were deeply planted in the soil of his farm. "Where would we go?"

"I'm consulting the Lord on that matter, as is your mother. You might try asking Him for suggestions yourself, daughter." He gave her a sidelong glance. "Anything on your mind these days?"

She studied her clasped hands, noting a torn fingernail. "Nothing I can talk about right now."

He sighed softly. "Well, when you're ready to talk, I'm ready to listen." He reached out to pat her cheek with his callused hand. "The Lord has a plan."

Instead of watching him leave, Marva gazed across the fields once more.

❧

That evening, after cleaning up the kitchen and after her parents had gone to bed, she sat down at the table and opened the newspaper. There had been no letters from Lucky since well before her trip up north. Her mind told her to stop looking, since finding nothing brought only hurt and frustration, yet her fingers turned the pages anyway.

The ad caught her eye almost instantly:

Dear Lonely in Longtree, This is a difficult letter to write, which is why I've been silent so long. I told you once before that God changed me, but you need to know how and why. As a young man, I fell into wild ways. Needing money to pay gambling debts, I stole cattle. By God's grace, I was not hanged for my crimes. I have paid my debts, but the stigma of prison will always be with me. If, after reading this, you still wish to correspond, I shall be forever grateful. If not, may the Lord's peace and blessings rest upon you. Ever yours, Lucky in Lakeland.

Marva read the note three times. Cattle rustling. A prison sentence. A vivid picture of a cold-eyed villain with a pock-marked face, an evil sneer, and prison pallor flashed through her thoughts. Lucky could look exactly like that Blanchard man at the cabin near Brandy Lake. He could smell even worse. He had never described his physical appearance, and she had never given hers.

A woman simply did not rush into marriage with a former convict. Even though the Lord had forgiven him, even though he was now a respected businessman—or so he said—he still might not make a good husband. Not for any woman. Particularly not for her.

What would her parents say? Papa was generally a kind-hearted man, but he had a tendency to be suspicious of former sinners. To his way of thinking, such men could never completely change. This viewpoint put man-made limits on God's powers of redemption and sanctification, which was entirely wrong, yet could anyone convince Papa of this? Not as yet. Not to Marva's knowledge.

Mother was more likely to think the best of people, yet she would follow her husband's lead. Much though she wanted her daughter to be happily married, she would no doubt blanch at the thought of a former convict for a son-in-law.

This knowledge gave Marva a measure of comfort. Parents were provided by God as sources of wisdom and protection from foolish choices. The very overprotectiveness she had disparaged for years might now prove useful.

Folding up the paper, she sat for a moment longer, her thoughts scattered. *Lucky. Prison. Monte?* No matter how often she tried to dispel the notion of Monte being Lucky as impossible, it kept returning.

With her thumb and forefinger, she tugged at her lower lip, struggling to remember. Hadn't Myles said something, years ago, about his older brother? Or had it been Virginia Van Huysen, Myles and Monte's grandmother? The dear old lady had loved to reminisce about her elder grandson to anyone who would listen, and Marva had often sat beside her in a rocking chair on Beulah's porch of a summer evening. But no, Virginia wouldn't have mentioned Monte's flaws; she had tended to dwell on the fact that he'd committed his life to the Lord before he died. That was understandable.

Pressing two fingers against her lips, Marva leaned back in her chair and stared out the kitchen window. Myles had run away from his grandmother's home to join the circus. Mrs. Van Huysen had sent Monte to find and bring back his little brother; he hadn't been involved in Myles's circus-performing days. From the circus, Myles had run out West. That ugly gray horse he used to ride, the one named after a cactus, had it come from Texas? She couldn't recall. Wherever it was, Monte had followed Myles someplace out West, and supposedly he had died in a cattle stampede.

Marva shook her head and dropped her fisted hands to her lap. This was no good. If Myles had ever mentioned Monte in connection with cattle rustling, she couldn't recall. She could ride over and visit Beulah tomorrow. . .but no. At the lodge, Beulah had refused to discuss Monte's past.

Leaving the newspaper behind, Marva slowly rose and climbed the steep stairs to her tiny bedroom above the kitchen.

Through her open windows flowed the familiar chorus of crickets, but tonight's show featured a solo performer—a lone cricket chirped from somewhere inside the room. It fell silent when she searched for it, naturally.

Two cats curled atop her coverlet. "What good are you?" she asked, smoothing the calico's soft fur. "Sleeping while a cricket roams the house." The cat rolled over and stretched without opening her eyes. Marva stroked the other cat's striped back and gently squeezed one white paw, but it never acknowledged her.

Her candle's light flickered over the sampler hanging above the head of her bed. Amid a field of faded flowers, crooked words stitched thirty years ago by her own hands proclaimed truth from Isaiah: "Thou wilt keep him in perfect peace, whose mind is stayed on thee: because he trusteth in thee."

Marva set her candleholder on the side table. "Peace," she whispered. Her eyes slowly closed. Sinking to her knees beside the bed, she flung her arms above her head and buried her face in her quilted coverlet. "I have no peace, Lord! I have no peace because I haven't trusted Thee. What shall I do? Oh, whatever shall I do!"

After the storm of emotion cleared, her knees began to ache. She sat back on her heels, then turned to sit with her back against the bed frame, rubbing her raised knees with both hands.

The cricket began to chirp again. The sound seemed to come from behind her dressing table.

"Lord God, I have no idea what to do next. I should answer Lucky's letter. . .but how? I cannot tell him that I'll marry him no matter what, because I don't even know if I want to marry him."

The truth rose in her thoughts, but she tried to squelch it.

"I know I should never have advertised for a husband. I don't know what I was think—Well, yes, actually I guess I do know. Rebellious thoughts, that's what I was thinking. I wanted to force Your hand. And now look what a mess I've made of things!"

She scrubbed her hands over her face. "The only man I want to marry is Monte Van Huysen. If he won't have me, I'll simply live out my days as a spinster. Maybe I'll find a widow or another spinster to set up housekeeping with me, and we'll be eccentric together and keep dozens of cats."

Her back began to ache. She climbed up on her bed, blew out her candle, pulled the striped cat into her lap, and stared out into darkness. As her eyes adjusted, the moonlit farmyard transformed into a magical world of shadows and light. An owl glided silently past the house and disappeared into a clump of trees.

"If Monte really is Lucky in Lakeland, then I do want to marry him, no matter if he does have a prison record in his past. I'll admit that much. I don't know if my parents will approve the match, but I know my own heart on that score, at least." She rubbed the cat around its ears and chin until a rumbling purr rewarded her efforts.

Did she truly know her own heart? A few weeks' acquaintance at a vacation lodge had provided sufficient time for her to develop a powerful attraction to the man, but did she know him well enough to pledge her love and fidelity for life? At times she thought she had glimpsed a depth of character behind his charming smile, but at other times he had seemed shallow. Physical attraction gave a relationship zest, for certain, yet a lifetime relationship required much more.

Remembering the solid strength of his arms, the warmth of his gaze, his gentle touch on her cheek. . .she lifted her hand to touch her face where he had once touched it. Disregarding the sleeping calico kitty, she flopped back against her feather bolster and tried to remember how it felt to rest against Monte's shoulder.

Love always involved risk. To love was to open one's heart to pain—the pain of loss, of rejection, of death. Was Monte Van Huysen worth such risk?

And what if all this speculation were baseless? What if Monte had never so much as seen her advertisement for a husband?

How can I know? How can I find out? I can scarcely ask Lucky in a public newspaper ad if he is Monte Van Huysen.

But to write a letter to Monte at the lodge. . . She dared not take so great a risk as that.

The calico cat, irritated by Marva's unrest, hopped off the bed.

"Lord God, please help me resolve this situation in a way that causes the least pain or embarrassment to everyone involved."

The cricket chirped.

Thump!

Marva's eyes opened wide.

Silence, then *crunch, crunch, crunch.*

Marva grimaced. "I did ask for that, didn't I? Thank you for doing your job, Patches." Still wrinkling her nose, she slid off the bed to change into her nightdress.

fourteen

Yea, all of you be subject one to another,
and be clothed with humility: for God resisteth the proud,
and giveth grace to the humble.
I Peter 5:5

"Crown Him with many crowns, the Lamb upon His throne." Marva sang along with the rest of the congregation while her fingers played the closing hymn. As soon as it ended, she picked up her book and her heavy shawl.

"You played the piano beautifully today, Marva. Thank you, as always, for serving so willingly. My hands are too stiff these days for me to do much playing, and Beulah and Myles have no time."

Marva looked into Violet Watson's smiling blue eyes and felt cheered. "I enjoy it, although I sometimes feel self-conscious. Myles plays so much better than I do."

Beulah's mother brushed that aside. "You do very well at accompanying while the congregation sings. Myles plays better than any of us, but if we depended on him for our music these days, we'd be in trouble. Beulah needs him to keep those boys in line during church services." Violet shook her head in mock despair, though evidently proud of her grandchildren.

Marva could think of nothing more to say. At one time she would have babbled on without thinking, but more often these days she found herself withdrawing into silence. She simply smiled and fell into step with the older woman as they exited the small church building.

Violet Fairfield Watson had remarried after her first husband's death, providing her three children, Beulah, Eunice, and Sam, with a loving stepfather. Obadiah and Violet Watson now had three sons of their own, all named for Old Testament prophets. Marva could never keep their names straight.

Obadiah Watson had served a long prison term for bank robbery, Marva recalled. But he had since been cleared of the crime, and the true criminal's identity had been discovered. Lucky, on the other hand, admitted that he had deserved *worse* than a prison sentence for his crimes.

Violet touched her arm. "Are you coming to Beulah's house for fellowship supper today? The pastor's family is joining us."

"Yes, I believe we're planning to come."

❧

The crowd at the Van Huysen farmhouse included the Spinellis, an Italian family who owned and operated the town's bakery, and the pastor and his large family. Children of all ages and sizes swarmed the premises inside and out, frequently slamming doors.

Beulah had baked a ham, and all the guests had brought food to share. The children filled their plates and sat outside on the porch chairs and steps. The adults clustered inside to partake of their meal, laughing and chatting.

Marva decided to fill her usual role and keep an eye on the children.

"Do you mind if I join you out here?" Caroline Schoengard let the screen door close behind herself.

"Please do. There's plenty of room." Marva smiled at the older woman.

Caroline pulled up another rocking chair beside her. "Since my incorrigible twins tend to start the most conflicts, I figure I'd better be responsible and prevent serious injuries, if possible."

"Are all of your children here today?"

"No, Scott, our oldest, is visiting his young lady friend over in Bolger."

Caroline nibbled at her food, but Marva sensed a question building. Sure enough, after setting down her fork, the pastor's wife asked, "So, did you enjoy our holiday in the Northwoods?"

"Yes, very much. I know my parents did as well. How about your family?"

"They all had the time of their lives. Even the girls enjoyed themselves. I believe we will attempt to make the trip again next year. I know it did my husband good to relax for a time. I worry about his health. His heart troubles him, you know."

"I hadn't realized that. I'm sorry to hear it," Marva said. "It is difficult for me to imagine Rev. Schoengard ill. He is always so vigorous."

"Well, we're all getting on in years."

Several of the larger boys started tossing a ball around and arguing among themselves. The little ones ran off behind the house to play. Two girls ran toward the barns, probably in search of kittens.

Marva pushed with her toes to rock her chair and enjoyed the temporary peace. It was a fine day with the crisp edge of autumn adding spice to the air. Some of the maples along the drive held touches of red.

The football game broke into shouting and accusations. Caroline rose and approached the porch rail. Cupping her hands around her mouth, she shouted for the boys to quiet down and behave like humans instead of beasts.

All those big boys wilted into submission, and their game resumed peacefully.

Caroline sat back down and gave Marva a self-conscious

smile. "I know I'm loud, but I've had to learn to project my voice to make myself heard."

"I'm impressed. All those large beings intimidate me," Marva confessed. "But I suppose a mother can't let herself be intimidated by her own sons."

Caroline laughed. Sobering, she gave Marva another sidelong glance. A nosy question was coming, and soon. What it would be, Marva could only guess.

"May I ask you a rather personal question?" Caroline asked. "I've been longing to ask it for a long time now. You'll probably think I'm silly, but. . .well, I'm not the only person who has wondered. Gossip is a sin, so I thought I would rather ask you directly than discuss the matter with anyone else."

"What is it?"

"You'll probably think I'm silly to ask, but. . ." Caroline sucked in a quick breath and let it out in a gust. "Awhile back—oh, many months ago—I saw an ad in the paper."

Oh, no.

Caroline chuckled and shook her head. "At first I thought it was a sales gimmick—you know how newspapers can be. But then. . .well. . . Oh, I'm messing this all up. You see, it was an advertisement from a single woman looking for a husband. My husband laughed about it at the time and teased that his daughters might try the same thing someday if it worked for this woman. None of us thought anything would come of it, but then there came an answer from a man."

She suddenly stopped and gave Marva a close look. "Have you seen the letters? Do you know what I'm talking about?"

"Yes, I've seen them."

"Oh, good. I thought you must have. People have talked about it off and on for a long time, but now more than ever. Have you seen the latest letter?"

"The one in which the man confesses his past? The prison sentence and all?"

Caroline nodded. "Isn't that heartrending? I've seen no answer from the woman yet. All of us are afraid she will turn him away now. One can hardly blame her, but still. . ."

Marva merely nodded. "What was it you wished to ask me?"

Caroline met her gaze for an instant, then laughed and shook her head. "You must think I'm crazy, but. . .many people in town believe that you are the woman who writes those letters. You're a Christian woman, and you live with your elderly parents on a farm—you fit her description exactly!"

Marva lowered her chin. "I can think of several other women who fit that description. Two or three even at our church."

"You're right, of course. . .but, oh well, it would have been so romantic! You're beautiful, so everyone immediately thought of how blessed that poor, lonely man would be to marry a woman like you. I mean, most of the other spinsters in this area aren't. . .well, they just aren't like you."

"Thank you. I had no idea. . . ."

Caroline chuckled. "You look years younger than any other woman your age, married or single. I think half the married women in the church are jealous of you. I know I am sometimes. By the time I was your age, I had lost my figure and my complexion."

"You were married with several children. That makes a difference."

"Perhaps. No one can understand why you've never married, Marva. Most people think you're too particular, but I disagree. Better for a woman to remain single than to marry in haste. The apostle Paul would uphold your position. I'll confess that David and I thought you and Monte Van Huysen made a striking couple, while we were up north, you know."

"Did you?" Marva smiled, hoping to appear amused by the notion.

"And when that most recent note appeared in the paper. . . well, one can't help adding two and two. Everyone acquainted with the Van Huysens knows the tragic story of Virginia's lost grandson, the prodigal who never got the chance to return. My fertile imagination immediately sprouted the notion that Monte must be Lucky in Lakeland. He's the right age, he owns a lodge on a lake, and the letters sound like him."

Caroline's anxious eyes studied Marva's face. "You undoubtedly think I'm crazy, coming up with this incredible romance for you. Once again, I appear to have added two and two incorrectly. Dave constantly tells me I must stop speculating about people and their business. I know he's right, but I can't seem to help myself."

Marva tried to end the conversation on a noncommittal note, but Caroline's words haunted her.

❧

Saturday night, Marva examined her reflection in her dressing table mirror, seeing the fine lines around her eyes and mouth, noting the deeper lines in her white neck. Silver blended almost unnoticeably with the gold of her hair. Deep blue eyes were her best feature by far. Although she had always worked to protect her complexion from the hot sun, her hands showed definite signs of wear and tear. Her figure, though far from ideal, was better now than it had been fifteen years earlier, since she no longer baked and ate many pastries and cakes, having long since given up on capturing a man with her cooking skills.

Would a man truly feel blessed to have her as his wife? Why

now, and not twenty years ago? Gazing into her reflected eyes, she recognized the changes God had worked on her heart over the past few months. Bitterness no longer lingered at the corners of her lips. Her expression held sorrow, mostly over the tangled results of her own headstrong behavior, yet hope brightened her eyes.

After church the next morning, she cornered the pastor's busy wife. "Caroline, you should be a sleuth," she said quietly.

Caroline stared at her blankly for a moment—then comprehension dawned. She clapped one hand over her mouth. Her shoulders began to shake. Giving up, she threw back her head and laughed heartily. "And you should be an actress! Marva Obermeier, you had me entirely convinced that I'd dived down the wrong rabbit hole." Eyes glowing, she gripped Marva's arm and whispered, "How right was I? Did you write those letters? Is Monte the man?"

"I wrote the Lonely letters, but I'm not sure about Monte. I need to answer Lucky's letter in a way only Monte could understand. I've been trying to work up enough courage. I've been thinking how to do it. Caroline, does everyone think I'm crazy? I'm so ashamed, so embarrassed for ever writing that first ad!"

"Nonsense." Caroline patted Marva's arm. "Everyone I've heard talking about the matter thinks it's the most romantic story they've ever heard. And if it should turn out to be Monte. . . Even Dave noticed the way Monte watched you while we were at his lodge. The entire company was buzzing about it."

"Buzzing." Marva repeated the word, her hands trembling. "Oh, Caroline, please pray for me. I don't want to do anything foolish again, trying to force God's hand."

"No one can force God's hand," Caroline said firmly. "Be

honest and true, and let Him handle the consequences." Her eyes began to twinkle again. "And tell me *every detail*!"

❧

Monte awaited his turn in the barber shop, listening with part of his brain to the other men discuss fishing and hunting successes and failures, but mostly pondering the fact that Lonely in Longtree had not yet replied to his confession.

In all his consideration of her possible responses, it had never entered his mind that she would refuse to answer at all. He wanted to believe that she was simply taking great pains with her response. But, then again, her taking such great pains would indicate a kind yet negative response. He sighed and folded his arms over his chest.

Whenever he worked up enough courage to pick up his mail today, he would probably find the latest edition of the Longtree paper. It might contain Marva's reply; it might not. Dread of yet another disappointment caused him to procrastinate.

He had promised Myles a visit during the autumn or early winter. A visit to Myles would entail attendance at his church, where an encounter with Marva was nearly inevitable.

If Marva turned him down, if she could not bear the shame of his past, he would prefer never to see her again, rather than torture himself with the unattainable. He might be obliged to explain this fact to his little brother, rather than risk wounding Myles and Beulah by breaking his promise with no explanation.

"Van Huysen, you're next." The barber waved him over.

❧

A short time later, Monte rode Petunia north on the Woodruff Road, his sober gaze fixed on nothingness. His saddlebags contained the day's mail, including a newspaper that he had not yet opened. He sensed it there behind him, waiting.

The autumn days were growing short and cold. Wind rippled Petunia's mane and tried to steal Monte's hat. He clapped it down more firmly on his head, then wriggled his fingers in his thick gloves. He and Hardy and the lodge staff had been busily storing boats and equipment for the long winter, sealing up the cabins and the lodge, and otherwise preparing for hibernation. Although Monte looked forward to free time for his writing, he dreaded months of loneliness.

"This is stupid," he told Petunia. "I'm putting myself through torture." He stopped the mare right there on the road, dismounted, and unpacked the newspaper from his saddlebag. He was obliged to remove one of his gloves in order to turn the pages.

Petunia turned to *whiffle* softly at the fluttering pages, then closed her eyes as if awaiting her master's pleasure.

Fighting the wind, squinting to read the newsprint by fading twilight, Monte scanned the page of ads. Then his entire body jerked. There it was, her reply. He looked away for a moment, almost unconsciously praying for strength.

> *Dear Lucky in Lakeland, Thank you for your honesty. Now that you have bared your soul, it seems only fair that I confess weaknesses of my own. I am overly sensitive to the sun's heat and to the ridicule of other people. I have a dread of unscheduled detours, yet I appreciate shadows of substance. If you can endure these peculiarities, perhaps we should plan to meet. Do you care for petunias? Lonely in Longtree.*

Monte crammed the unfolded paper into his saddlebag, wrapped his arms around Petunia's neck, and buried his face in her mane. A few minutes later, he spun around and whooped.

Calming and catching his startled horse consumed a few extra minutes of his time, but he was too happily distracted to care.

fifteen

If any of you lack wisdom, let him ask of God,
that giveth to all men liberally, and upbraideth not;
and it shall be given him.
JAMES 1:5

Marva stepped out of the chicken pen and latched its gate. The basket on her arm held few eggs. This cold weather discouraged the hens from laying, even though they were snug inside the barn.

One of the cows lowed plaintively. The farm always seemed quiet and peaceful as autumn advanced toward winter. Last week had been hectic, what with slaughtering the pigs and all the work involved in that unpleasant chore. No matter how much she enjoyed eating sausages, Marva intensely disliked making them.

"Miss Marva?"

She tried not to reveal her surprise. J. D. Parker had a way of appearing out of nowhere. The hired man approached her from the stanchions where the milk cows licked up the last of their evening feed.

"Yes, Mr. Parker?" She smiled. J. D. was stocky in build, nearly bald, yet rather nice looking.

He twisted his cap between his large hands, and his face turned an unbecoming red. "I know this is bold of me, but I've discussed it with your father, and he's agreeable if you are. I'd like to marry you, ma'am. It would be a good thing for everyone involved. Your parents could stay on with us in the house as long as they live. You and I would make a good partnership."

Marva felt as if she were watching the little scene from somewhere far away. She stared at Parker's earnest face until he looked away in confusion. "Meaning no insult, ma'am. I thought—I hoped—you might approve the idea."

With an effort, she gathered her senses. "I am not insulted, Mr. Parker. I simply. . .I had never considered such a thing. You say my parents have approved?"

He nodded, his gray eyes lighting up. "I'll not press you for an answer, Miss Marva. We've time to consider." He bobbed an awkward little bow and made his escape.

Marva returned to the house as if in a trance. Marry J. D. Parker? Her parents wanted her to marry him?

While she prepared the evening meal, Marva pondered this unexpected turn of events. Her parents chatted comfortably to each other, apparently unaware of their daughter's inner turmoil. During supper she picked at her food, feeling J. D.'s frequent glances from across the table. As soon as he finished eating, he excused himself and stepped outside. He never stayed for Papa's nightly Bible reading.

Thinking of J. D.'s proposal, of all that marriage to him would certainly entail, gave her an inward shudder. Nice man though he was, she had no interest whatsoever in giving herself to him as a wife. At one time she might have snapped up his offer, considering it the best chance she was likely to receive. At one time she had been foolish.

But then again, had she ever actually been that foolish? Over the years she had discouraged the attentions of many would-be swains. Always her heart had continued to hope that somewhere out there in the great world existed at least one man whom she could respect and love without reserve.

Was she being unfair to J. D.? Although he attended church regularly, she had no idea what he believed about God and salvation. He was also rough with the animals at times, demonstrating a lack of patience and kindness.

Papa closed his Bible, and Marva realized she had not listened to one word. While he led in prayer, she closed her eyes and had her own private conversation with the Lord.

Please guide me, Lord. I am terribly confused! I have pleaded with Thee for wisdom and guidance, but I've heard no answer. I don't know what to do!

Papa shoved back his chair and patted his stomach. "Another excellent meal, daughter. Nothing like fresh pork chops." Something crackled in the bib of his overall. He paused and reached into the pocket, pulling out a folded, crumpled letter. "Ah, forgot about this."

She reached to take the letter he held out to her.

"It came the other day, and I plumb forgot about it. I ask your pardon for an old man's faulty memory."

Marva glanced up from her perusal of the unfamiliar handwriting on the envelope long enough to smile at her father. "Of course, Papa. I'm just as forgetful as you are."

"Who is it from, Marva?" Mother asked.

"I'm not sure. I'll read it after I clean up the kitchen." She had no desire to read her unexpected letter under her parents' curious eyes.

Although she didn't like to suspect them of inordinate curiosity, Papa and Mother did seem to stay up past their usual bedtime hour. Once, while she swept the kitchen floor, she caught her mother watching her with an expectant look. "What's the matter?" Marva paused to ask.

Mother waffled for a moment, then said in carefully casual

tones, "I was simply wondering when you planned to read your letter."

"Probably after I go upstairs." Hearing a *meow*, she opened the outer door to let in two waiting cats. They rubbed about her ankles while she hung up the dishtowels to dry over the stove. After giving each one a small plate of minced pork chop, she squatted down to pet her kitties while they ate.

Before she headed upstairs, she kissed her parents good night. Her mother wore a fixed expression as if trying to appear unconcerned. "Good night, dear." Even her voice sounded restrained.

Marva caught her father giving her mother a warning look, but he instantly switched it to a fond smile as she bent over him. "Good night, Papa."

"Good night, my Marva."

The cats followed her upstairs and laid claim to the bed. Her bedchamber was cold. She probably should have brought up a hot brick for her feet, but she hadn't thought ahead to warm one. Shivering, she set her candle and the letter on her bedside table and deliberately prepared for bed. She took down her hair, brushed it, braided it, and tucked it beneath her nightcap. Wearing woolen socks with her flannel nightgown, she slipped beneath her coverlet and two quilts. The cats immediately curled up at her sides like two purring hot-water bottles.

At last she reached for her letter and tore open the envelope. Rising to lean on one elbow, she tilted the page so that the candlelight fell upon it.

Dear Marva,

I hope I do not offend by addressing you so, but in truth, you are inestimably dear to me. Your recent letter in the Enquirer *with its clever allusions to our adventures together fills me with hope that my suit is not entirely abhorrent to you. Can you truly forgive and forget my wicked past and accept me as a new man in Jesus Christ? I would have spoken many times while you graced my lodge with your lovely presence, and I would have revealed my identity as your newsprint admirer—had not fear held me in its grip—fear of your rejection if you knew me for what I am. I do not know how long ago you guessed my identity as your devoted Lucky in Lakeland. I guessed—I hoped—you might prove to be my Lonely in Longtree that first evening when I met you at my brother's cabin.*

Already I was fond of you in print. Never had I imagined that my hoped-for bride would be as beautiful as a man's daydreams! How often have I invented for my fictional heroes lovely heroines whose descriptions closely match yours. I laugh to think of it. How well God knows my heart!

Does your letter indicate that you forgive my cowardice, my foolish attempt at deception? Is it possible that you return my regard? Is it possible, dare I dream that your parents might accept one such as I as their son-in-law? I can hardly eat or sleep for mixed dread and urgency to learn your reply.

I could write paeans to your beauty and grace—in fact, I have written them, and they lay crumpled around my feet. Lest I annoy you with rapturous expressions of devotion, I herein attempt to be sparing of words and simply ask the questions that weight my soul.

Soon I shall travel to your town to visit my brother and his family. Although I eagerly anticipate my visit with them, my true heart's desire is to be with you again, to deepen our acquaintance into friendship and more—much more.

I demand nothing of you, beloved; I have no right. I simply lay my heart at your feet and humbly implore you to take me as your husband.

Yours always,
Montague Van Huysen

PS I am extraordinarily fond of one particular Petunia.

Marva read the letter through several times. It was true! Her fondest dream was actually true! How could this be? Dare she believe that all these years her heart had waited for this one man to enter her life? That God had caused her to wait in solitude while He prepared Monte Van Huysen to become her husband?

But this was not the time for deep introspection; this was the time to revel in his admiration and love. And his beautiful writing! How many men of her acquaintance could express their feelings with such poetic grace?

None other. Not even one.

Monte wants to marry me! He thinks I'm beautiful!

Smiling, laughing, and crying, she hugged her cats and gave whispered thanks to the Lord. Long into the night she lay awake, thinking and dreaming and wondering. What would he do? When would he come? Would he insist upon a proper courtship, or would he ask for a quick wedding? Which would be better?

But when morning dawned, doubts and indecision crept back into her heart. The main question was the one Monte had asked: Would her parents accept him? They had seemed to like him well enough at the lodge, but Monte as expert fishing guide and genial host was a vastly different proposition from Monte the ex-convict as a prospective son-in-law.

She did her morning chores distractedly, sometimes drifting off in thought until a protesting *moo* or a lashing tail brought her back to reality. While watching her chapped hands draw milk from a cow's pendulous udder, she recognized the irony of her current dilemma.

J. D. Parker offered exactly the kind of marriage she had decided to settle for back when she wrote that original ad—a loveless business partnership designed to keep the farm in Marva's family. But she no longer desired that kind of marriage. How had she ever imagined that such an arrangement would satisfy her needs? Blind stubbornness and disrespect for God had brought her to make such foolish choices.

Although Parker had worked around the farm since early summer, she scarcely knew the man and felt no attachment to him whatsoever. As far as she could tell, he had no feelings for her either. His interest lay entirely in the farm; proposing marriage to Marva was simply a necessary step in obtaining possession of her family's property.

Hearing a *mew*, she turned to see Patches and Tigress watching her hopefully. With a smile, she squirted a little milk in their direction and watched the cats lick it from each other's fur. Funny creatures.

Rising, she patted Annabelle's bony hip and lifted the full pail. The elderly shorthorn still produced a fine calf every year, and her milk production rivaled that of younger cows. "Good ol' girl."

Marva lugged the pail toward the milk room, where sloshing noises indicated that J. D. Parker was hard at work. The cats followed at her heels, cleaning up any involuntary spills.

The top of Mr. Parker's head reflected lamplight as he bent over a milk can. He looked up at Marva's approach and set down an empty bucket.

"Here, let me take that."

Marva handed over her full pail and watched J. D. empty it into the can. Patches hurried to lick up a puddle near the can, but J. D. shoved the cat away with his boot. "Git."

Marva scooped up her insulted kitty for a cuddle. What would it harm to let the cats clean up spills? They earned their keep on the farm by keeping rodent populations down.

Most of the birds and beasts raised on a farm would someday be killed for food, yet Papa treated his animals with kindness as long as they lived. Whenever he was obliged to slaughter a beast, he always dispatched it as quickly and painlessly as possible. Although Parker was never cruel to the animals, he showed little regard for their comfort or feelings.

A sudden memory of Monte's mare resting her head on his shoulder while he rubbed her ears and murmured nonsensical sweet talk brought a smile to her face. Monte would appreciate her cats, she felt certain, and they would like him.

Was she making excuses for her possibly selfish decision to choose Monte over Mr. Parker? Emotions could easily blind a woman's heart to wisdom. She needed wise and objective counsel, but where could she find such a thing?

❧

Holding his carpetbag in one hand, Monte stepped onto the crowded station platform. The little town of Longtree was busier than he had expected. No one greeted him at the station, since he had sent Myles no definite date of arrival. Rather than crowd into his brother's house, he had decided to lodge in town.

Stopping a gentleman on the street, he inquired, "Can you recommend a hotel or boardinghouse?"

"Certainly, sir. Amelia Martin runs the best place in town."

Monte followed the stranger's directions and soon found

himself at a neat establishment located on a side street. The proprietress, an angular, gray-haired woman wearing a stiffly starched apron over a baggy gown, showed him to a small but immaculate bedchamber. "Dinner is served at six in the dining room." Her voice was incongruously deep. "Don't be late if you want to eat."

After the door closed behind her with a sharp click, Monte unpacked his bag and hung his clothes on wall hooks. Kicking off his shoes, he stretched out on the bed, folded his hands behind his head, and regarded the ceiling. Although no coherent requests passed through his mind, let alone his lips, a constant prayer rose from the depths of his spirit.

When he arrived downstairs at precisely six, men of varied descriptions filled the dining room with rumbling voices and nearly overpowering body odor. Most of these diners would not be residents of the boardinghouse, he deduced. Women were noticeably absent from their number. He pulled out a chair between a natty salesman-looking type and a sweat-stained laborer with shaggy hair and beard.

Mrs. Martin and an elderly man called Boz waited on the table. Boz had full use of only one arm, yet he managed to carry platters and bowls of food, pour drinks, and otherwise satisfy his customers. Monte soon guessed that Boz was husband to Mrs. Martin.

The food was excellent, and the dinner conversation offered nearly as much information as a scan of the weekly newspaper. Monte heard many familiar names, including his brother's, during the course of the meal.

"Listen up! I got news."

Everyone, including Monte, gazed toward the far end of the table, where a man with a large red nose tapped on his glass with his spoon. "I just come from the Shamrock, where

J. D. Parker bought drinks all around 'cuz he's fixin' to get married."

The man seated next to him shook his head. "I heard that tale, too, but the fact is, she ain't given J. D. no answer yet. Ask me, and I'd say he's counting his chickens too soon."

"Who's the woman?" another man called from Monte's end of the table.

"Marva Obermeier," answered Red Nose.

Monte's fork stopped halfway to his open mouth.

"Eh, he's good as married. That woman's been desperate to catch a man for twenty years." Bitterness laced the speaker's voice.

"If that's so, why'd she turn you down, Nugget?" someone else shouted, earning raucous and mocking laughter.

Recovering his poise, Monte laid down his fork and took a sip of water.

"And you, Buff. I hear you proposed to her once."

"That was ten years ago. I reckon most of us have made a try for her and her farm at some time or other," the burly farmhand at Monte's left admitted.

"I heard tell she advertised for a husband in the paper."

"That was a sales gimmick," another voice said in scoffing tones. "Face it, Marva could take her pick of us if she weren't so particular. If J. D. wins her, he's one lucky fellow."

Amelia Martin burst into the room, leaned over, and smacked a platter of bread on the table. "Enough of your gossip," she snapped. "And they say women talk too much!"

Monte took a bite of buttered bread but found it difficult to swallow.

sixteen

And this I pray, that your love may abound yet more and more in knowledge and in all judgment.
PHILIPPIANS 1:9

"Mr. Parker, may I have a word with you?" Marva hoped he would attribute the quiver in her voice to the morning chill. Hands clutching at her shawl, she watched him load a full milk can into the wagon.

He immediately hopped down and faced her, rubbing his gloved hands on his thighs. His quick breath steamed from his smiling mouth. "Anytime." Bold admiration glistened in his pale eyes.

"This will take only a moment of your time, actually." She squared her shoulders and forged ahead. "After much prayer and consideration, I have determined that I must refuse your flattering offer of marriage."

He stared at her without blinking. She saw his hands close into fists. "Why?"

"I have already given my heart to another man. If he will not marry me, I shall remain single."

Tight lips and an angry glare revealed the man's feelings. "Who?" he finally asked through clenched teeth.

"I cannot see how that information is your concern, sir. I appreciate the honor you gave me by requesting my hand in marriage, but such an arrangement would never work." With a quick nod, she turned back toward the house.

His hand closed over her upper arm, stopping her short. Sensing his vastly superior strength, she turned to stare at him, her throat closing in fear.

"I'll not stay on this farm as a hired hand. Tell your father either you marry me or he sells the place to me or I leave." Anger glittered in Parker's red-rimmed eyes.

Marva nodded.

He released her and turned away.

❧

Tension stretched a long silence to the snapping point. Marva chewed a tiny bite of chicken and had to wash it down with a quick gulp of milk. Parker's sullen stare from across the supper table made her flesh creep. No matter what her parents might say, she did not regret refusing his proposal.

At last Papa laid his napkin across his plate and reached back to pull the Bible from its shelf. Before he could open it, Parker pushed back his chair and spoke.

"Unless you'll sell this place to me, Obermeier, I'll be pulling out in the next few days."

Papa laid the Bible on the table and folded his hands atop it. "I see no reason why we cannot discuss terms of sale. Shall we set up a time to meet tomorrow at the bank?" He spoke with unaccustomed formality.

Parker's aggressive manner dissolved into pleased surprise. "Yes, sir, that would be right fine with me."

"After dinner, shall we say?"

"After dinner," Parker agreed. "You are serious? You'll consider selling out?"

"I'll certainly consider your offer, Mr. Parker."

Smiling, the hired man rose and excused himself. To Marva's relief, he did not glance her way. "I'll check the stock once more before I head to town."

"You have always been dependable and hardworking, Parker. Thank you." Papa rose to shake Parker's hand before the hired man departed.

As soon as the door closed behind him, Mother let out her breath in a long and noisy sigh. "Oh, Gustaf, how marvelous! Thank the Lord!" She suddenly covered her face with a handkerchief.

Marva stared in startled consternation. "Mother?"

Her mother lowered the handkerchief to reveal her smiling face. "Such a relief! Oh, thank God! I was so afraid you would agree to marry that man, Marva. He asked your father's permission to propose marriage to you, and we feared you would accept him out of desperation. How I have prayed that you would be wise!"

Papa snorted softly. "I told you to have faith in our daughter's good sense. Parker is not a bad man, but why should Marva marry him?"

Mother leaned forward, her intense gaze holding Marva captive. "Years ago, Papa and I promised each other never again to interfere in your matters of the heart, but I never expected to find it so difficult to keep that promise! When you advertised for a husband in the newspaper, I thought I should die of shock."

"You knew?"

"Not at first," Papa answered. "But over time we figured it out."

"Always we hoped you would confide in us," Mother said, her tone reproachful. "We might have helped in your search for Lucky while we stayed at the lodge."

"Although, as it turns out, we found him for you on our first attempt," Papa added with a grin. "I suspected he might advertise his lodge in our newspaper for a reason. Never guessed about his being Myles's lost brother, of course. To be honest, I thought Mr. Stowell was the man at first. I didn't know about his partner."

"Dearest, why are you tormenting that man?" Mother asked. "Have you answered his letter? His past is disgraceful, to be sure, but the Lord has changed him into a man whom any woman should be justly proud to wed."

Marva could hardly speak. "How long have you known?"

"We figured things out sooner than you did," Mother said, reaching across the table to pat Marva's hand. "Probably because we could observe the matter more objectively. Both Mr. Stowell and Mr. Van Huysen admired you from the first, but Mr. Van Huysen had an air of purpose about him."

"Purpose mixed with fear." Papa frowned. "I didn't understand the fear until I read his confession in the newspaper."

"You know he is truly a man of God now, don't you, Papa?" Marva asked.

"Had I not come to know and respect him prior to his confession, I would have been reluctant to admit such a change would be possible. This old man has learned a lesson about God's redemptive power. It galls me to marry my only daughter to an ex-convict, yet at the same time, I am proud to marry my only daughter to a godly man and famous author. I believe he will make you happy."

Mother smiled and shook her head. "Happy is too weak a word. Such joy I found in seeing a fine man look upon our daughter with love and devotion in his eyes! And to know that she returns his love!" She heaved another ecstatic sigh. "God's ways are always best."

"But now what shall we do?" Marva asked. "I have not yet answered his letter because I did not know what to say. Yes, I love him and wish to marry him, but I cannot simply hop on a train and travel north."

Papa nodded decidedly. "Leave that to me, child. I'll write to inform Mr. Van Huysen of our plans to sell the farm and move north."

"You plan to move north, too?"

Her parents appeared surprised by her question. "But of course," Papa said. "We have been discussing this for months—ever since our summer vacation. The winters up north might be harsher than winters here, but there we might remain indoors in a luxurious lodge, read, and visit with our daughter and her husband. What more could a lazy old couple like us desire?"

"We shall come with you and accept your Mr. Van Huysen's proposal. I've been sorting through possessions these past months, preparing for a move," Mother said in her practical way.

Marva's gaze shifted back and forth between their beloved faces as her thoughts scrambled to catch up. Laughter built inside her until it spilled out in a hearty peal. "You darlings! How sneaky you are!"

❧

"We're home!"

Marva hurried to the door to greet her parents. "How did the meeting go?"

"Quite well," Papa said, letting her take his muffler and hang it on a wall hook.

Before he could say another word, Mother inserted, "Marva, guess who we saw in town—Monte Van Huysen!"

Marva paused with her mouth ajar, then gathered her thoughts enough to respond, "Oh."

"He apparently arrived the day before yesterday, and of course he's been at his brother's house to visit, although he is staying at the Martins' boardinghouse." Mother's eyes snapped with excitement. "He stopped your father and—" Her flow of words cut off suddenly, and she gave her husband an apologetic glance. "But Papa can tell you. . . ."

Papa finished hanging up his coat and Mother's. Then, placing his arm around Marva's shoulders, he walked beside her into the kitchen. "He asked if he might call on us this afternoon."

"Today?" Marva's throat nearly closed with a combination of panic and joy.

"You'd best tidy yourself before he arrives," Mother suggested. "The bread smells wonderful, and you baked apple kuchen as well, did you not?"

"I'll brew fresh coffee," Papa volunteered.

Marva changed into her blue dimity frock, the most becoming of her gowns, though rather light for the season. Seated at her dressing table, she fussed with her hair, pulling wisps down to wave in front of her ears. Her cheeks were rosy, her eyes bright.

Could a woman die of love? For the first time, she believed it possible.

❧

The sheen of frost coated grass and trees. Monte's breath froze on his scarf, and his hired horse's breath beaded its whiskers. *Clop, clop, clop.* It trotted along a country road, carrying him ever closer to Marva, ever closer to his future.

The Obermeier farm looked much like every other farm in southern Wisconsin. The barn was in need of repair, and the paint on the house's porch had peeled off in strips; yet overall the place wore an air of comfort. His horse whinnied, and a cart horse in the corral answered.

Smoke trickled from the chimney. Although the farmyard

appeared deserted, he knew Marva and her parents were at home. He dismounted and wrapped his mount's reins around a post.

His boots clunked on the steps, and his own breathing seemed noisy. Now that the moment had arrived, his brain felt wooden.

After closing his eyes to pray silently for strength, he knocked on the door.

He heard footsteps inside. A bolt slid back, and the door opened to reveal Mr. Obermeier. "Come in, Mr. Van Huysen, and welcome. Hang your hat and coat on these hooks. My wife will be grateful if you will scrape your boots."

The greeting seemed restrained. Monte could read nothing in the older man's expression. At their meeting in town that afternoon and always during his stay at the lodge, Mr. Obermeier had seemed friendly. Now he exuded dignity and detachment.

Delightful aromas of cinnamon, yeast, and coffee wafted through the house.

Mrs. Obermeier appeared from the kitchen. "We're so thankful you found time to visit us, Mr. Van Huysen. Our Marva has baked *apfel* kuchen, and we've prepared fresh coffee. I hope you can stay for supper as well."

If his plans went smoothly, he shared that hope. If not. . .

"Come on into the kitchen where it's warm." Mrs. Obermeier beckoned him forward. Her manner, at least, was reassuringly unchanged.

As he entered the room, Marva straightened and turned to place a steaming loaf on a wire rack. "Good evening, Mr. Van Huysen."

"Good evening, Miss Obermeier."

After giving him a shy smile, she draped the dish towels she had used to protect her hands over a bar on the oven door and removed her apron.

"Please be seated. I'll pour the coffee and serve up the apple cake."

The minutes seemed to drag. Monte did his best to engage in small talk with her parents, mostly about his relatives, yet he felt acutely aware of Marva's presence. "Ginny took her first steps the other day. Beulah tried to make her walk to me, but she would only walk away from me to her mother."

"How quickly these children grow!" Mrs. Obermeier observed, giving her own daughter a fond glance, as if Marva were taking her first steps. Monte found this glimpse of maternal affection both amusing and appealing.

Once Marva had served coffee and cake to everyone, she took her seat across the table from him. He found himself caught between the desire to watch her, to drink in her beauty, and the need to conceal his fascination from her parents. The small talk continued while they ate. Monte burned his tongue on his coffee. Marva crumbled her cake with her fork and ate little of it.

Mr. Obermeier cleared his throat. "As we informed you earlier, Mr. Van Huysen, my wife and I were at the bank today to discuss the impending sale of our farm. Our hired man has offered to buy it."

"J. D. Parker?"

"Why, yes. How do you know his name?" Mr. Obermeier lifted one bushy white brow.

"Talk around the table at the boardinghouse the other night concerned his plans to marry into the Obermeier family."

"Well, of all the nerve!" Marva snapped.

Monte met her irate gaze, trying not to smile in relief. "One can hardly blame a man for trying."

She huffed, but he saw her lips twitch. "He proposed, but I turned him down. He told me my parents wanted me to marry him, which not only confused me but was also false. I could never have married him under any circumstances."

He studied her guileless blue eyes. "I'm glad to hear it."

Her cheeks flushed, and she looked away.

Mr. Obermeier linked his hands together and set them before him on the table with an air of importance. "Our daughter tells us you have made her a proposal of marriage as well."

Monte's throat tightened again. "Yes, sir, I have."

"We are also aware of the newspaper correspondence you have pursued these past two years. In your most recent post, you mentioned a prison sentence in your past. Before I give a yea or nay to your proposal, I would hear your story."

Monte saw Marva give her father a startled glance, and his hopes took a downturn. He cleared his throat and shifted on his chair. "It is not a pleasant story, sir, and I take no pleasure in repeating it."

"Perhaps this will be the last time repetition will prove needful," Mr. Obermeier said, his pale eyes offering neither reprieve nor condemnation.

"Myles and I both worked for a cattle outfit owned by Cass Murdoch in Texas. It was hard work with decent pay and lots of adventure. But I—I fell into bad company. Very bad company. I did things I don't ever want to think about."

He could not look up from his coffee cup. Shame burned his face. These inescapable memories galled him always; to relate them to Marva and her parents was more painful than he had imagined.

"God listened to my grandmother's prayers. He gave me no peace. I was miserable all the time. Nothing gave me pleasure.

Finally, I attended a camp meeting in the next town and heard an evangelist preach about Christ's death on the cross and His resurrection. I'd heard the story all my life, knew it by heart, yet that time God skewered me with it. I walked up the aisle and prayed with the minister. I can't describe the relief I felt when I handed my worthless life over to God."

seventeen

My beloved spake, and said unto me,
Rise up, my love, my fair one, and come away.
SONG OF SOLOMON 2:10

Monte's voice broke. Mrs. Obermeier pressed a handkerchief into his hand, but he blinked hard and controlled his emotions.

"At first I didn't know what to do. I told Myles what God had done for me; I gave him a Bible so he could read for himself, but at the time he wasn't grateful. I know he was ashamed to call me his brother, and he had every reason to feel that way.

"A no-good gambler named Jeb Kirkpatrick was after my hide. I had owed him a bundle of money for months, and he knew I didn't have the cash. Always before when I got into gambling debt, I'd rustle a few head of beef. But since I gave my life to God, I knew stealing wasn't the answer to my problem. I kept praying, asking the Lord to show me what to do, and all the time, Jeb kept getting madder and more insistent that I pay up.

"One night, I was riding watch over the herd, all the while fighting my green-broke mustang. Jeb and his gang came riding up and demanded the cash. I told him I would have to make payments to him out of my salary. His antipathy to the plan was evidenced by the way he hauled out a gun and shot me. I'd be dead right now if my horse hadn't reared up and dropped me off. The cattle stampeded. I got stepped on at least once before I rolled into a ravine and hid."

Marva reached across the table and took his hand. "Myles thought you were dead," she said.

He nodded. "I didn't know it at the time, but Myles saw the scene from a distance. After the stampede, he came looking for me, didn't find me, and thought I'd been trampled to dust, I guess. He thought I was dead. I thought he left Texas because he never wanted to see me again. It took us twenty years and more to get our stories straight."

"What a shame!" said Mrs. Obermeier. "But how did you keep alive?"

"The next thing I remember is waking up in an Indian's house. Not a tepee, but a house made of bricks. It was a family of Apaches—a man, his wife, two small children, and an old woman."

"Surely not Apaches," Mr. Obermeier interrupted. "They're the most savage of all Indian tribes. At least, so I've read. . . ."

"In Dutch Montana's books," Marva finished his sentence.

"And other places," her father defended himself.

Monte suddenly felt more relaxed. "They were Apaches right enough, and some of the most Christlike people I've met in all my days. The man spoke English and could read. A missionary had given him a Bible. He shared it with me while I stayed with them.

"I did some deep thinking while my wounds were healing. God started nagging me about all the stealing I had done. I read in the Bible where God wanted thieves to pay back what they had stolen—to make restitution. So as soon as I was back on my feet, I returned to Murdoch, my boss, and confessed. It wasn't an easy thing to do, but it was the right thing. Since I owned up, Murdoch was merciful. I spent two years locked up."

"How awful for you!" Marva said just above a whisper. "Yet it was the right thing to do."

Monte nodded. "While I was behind bars, Jeb Kirkpatrick and his gang were caught rustling, and some vigilantes lynched them on the spot."

"Lynched?" Mrs. Obermeier inquired.

"It means a hanging without a trial," her husband said, his tone grim.

"Had I been caught rustling, I would have been strung up alongside the others."

"God's plans for your life helped put a stop to your wild ways just in time." Marva's gentle squeeze of his hand lifted his spirits.

"Did you ever make restitution to your boss?" Mr. Obermeier asked.

"As soon as I got out of jail, I started working off my debt. It took more than two years to pay for the cattle I'd helped steal, and then Murdoch kept me on for another year after that. I talked with him a lot about God, and he started attending church with me. His wife and daughter became believers, and then the boss did, too. Not long afterwards, I cut loose and headed north."

"Leaving all your friends behind?" Marva asked.

"It was time. I thought of hunting for Myles but hadn't a clue where to start looking. No one knew where he'd headed. I thought of returning to New York, but I wanted to wait until. . .well, until I had made something of myself. I was too proud to go back with my pockets empty. Stupid, I know, but that's how I felt."

"And that was when you went to Wyoming and became a hunting guide and then started writing books?"

Monte nodded, grateful for Marva's conclusion to his tale.

A short silence fell. Monte studied Marva's strong, white fingers wrapped around his. The connection gave him comfort.

Her father cleared his throat. "Well, well. Thank you, Mr. Van Huysen, for sharing your story. I am certain it was not easy for you, but I believe the truth needed airing. To be sure, if anyone but you had told me such a drastic change in a man's life was possible, I would have scoffed. So often I have witnessed these dramatic conversions that later come to naught. . . . But yours is obviously genuine."

Monte did not know how to respond to this. He simply nodded, holding the old man's gaze.

"Since your present reputation is built upon twenty years of honest living and hard work, Mrs. Obermeier and I give our approval to your suit. Why don't you two go on into the parlor where you can propose in private? We'll stay here." Just as Monte and Marva started to rise, he added, "However, we believe a proper engagement period should be observed, since you've spent little time together in person."

"Yes, sir." Stepping to the end of the table, Monte gripped his future father-in-law's hand. "And thank you, sir."

Mrs. Obermeier pulled Monte's head down and kissed his cheek. "She'll make you happy, Monte."

He returned her teary-eyed smile. "And I'll do my best to make her happy, ma'am."

❧

Carrying a lamp, Marva led the way to the parlor as if walking in a dream. A rush of cold air met them as Monte reached around her to push open the door. She stepped inside and set the lamp on one of her mother's hand-carved walnut tables.

"This room isn't very comfortable," she said in apology.

"We shouldn't need to stay long." He caught her shoulders

and turned her to face him. "I've got to do this thing right." He lowered himself to one knee and took her hand. "Marva Obermeier, my dear Lonely in Longtree, will you marry me and allow me to end your loneliness?"

Clutching his hand with both of hers, she laughed with a catch in her voice. "Yes, oh yes!"

"Then I shall truly be Lucky in Lakeland." Using the sofa for support, he climbed back to his feet. "That going down on one knee is not as easy as it should be." He took both her hands in his and turned her so the candlelight revealed her features. Gently he caressed the line of her jaw. "You are so lovely. I cannot tell you how grateful I am to the Lord for keeping you for me, for only me!"

Joy filled Marva's heart so full that she could not speak.

"May I kiss you?" he asked in a whisper.

She nodded. Her legs shook until she feared they would give way beneath her.

Slowly he leaned forward. His mustache brushed her cheek, and then his lips touched hers in a chaste kiss. Marva looked up into his dark eyes, wanting another kiss but too shy to ask. His hands slid up her arms to grip her shoulders, and he kissed her cheek, then her temple. With a little groan, he wrapped his arms around her shoulders and pulled her against him. "Marva, I love you so very much."

Growing bolder, Marva slipped her hands around his waist and listened to his heart beating against her ear. "I love you, Monte." Being in his arms felt so strange, yet so right.

He swallowed hard. "How—how long is a proper engagement period? Are we talking weeks? Months?"

"I don't know. Shall we ask my father?"

"I don't want to head back north without you, but I can't leave Hardy with all the work for too long." He pressed his cheek to the top of her head.

She squeezed his waist. "I don't want to be left behind."

They held each other for another minute or two before he admitted, "I can hardly bear to let go of you."

"I know." With her face against his chest, she nodded, smiling yet serious.

"We'd better go talk to your parents before they come looking for us." He took her by the hand, gazing once more into her eyes, then picked up the candle and led her from the room.

Marva's parents turned expectant faces their way as they entered the kitchen. "Your daughter has just promised to marry me," Monte said, his voice hoarse. He had to clear his throat.

"Then we can start making plans," Papa said, sounding nearly as gruff. "What do you say to marrying in December? Can you stay in the area that long?"

Monte's grip on Marva's hand tightened. "Yes, sir, I can make that work."

"Good. That gives us plenty of time to sell this place and pack up to move north. I am assuming your offer of a home for your wife's parents still stands? I seem to recall such an offer early on in your newspaper correspondence with our daughter." Papa's eyes held a subtle twinkle.

Monte grinned weakly. "It still stands, sir. She told you about that, eh?"

"Marva didn't have to tell us," Mother said quickly. "We figured it out. I cannot tell you how hard it was to keep my mouth shut while we were in Minocqua! You two and your secrets." She sniffed, but her smile took any sting from her words.

❧

"You are so lovely, my dear." Mother smoothed Marva's hair

over her ear and stepped back to admire. "That deep blue brings out your eyes."

"I hope Mr. Van Huysen approves of my appearance." Marva felt suddenly shy and uncertain.

"I am certain he will approve. If he does not, he knows nothing of fashion." Mother touched the piped trim at Marva's wrist and nodded in satisfaction. "Men seldom notice a woman's attire anyway. He will focus on your face. Smile, child. You've caught yourself a fine man."

Marva bridled. "I did not catch him, Mother. I wrote the first letter, but ever since then, he has pursued me. I was careful to leave matters entirely in his hands."

Mother patted her hand. "Calm yourself; it is merely an expression. I am well aware that you have learned to put such matters into the Lord's keeping, since I have been learning the same lesson. I always longed for my daughter to experience happiness with the right man, but only because I love you so dearly."

Relaxing, Marva tried to smile. "I know, Mother. Had I met Mr. Van Huysen twenty years ago, he would have broken my heart. The Lord's timing is perfect."

"Amen."

Marva turned at the sound of her father's voice. "Papa, you look so handsome in your best suit." It was slightly threadbare at the cuffs, but no one would notice.

"*Hmph.* Are you ready? The others are waiting."

"I am ready, Papa."

Her parents escorted her into the magistrate's office, where Monte waited along with Myles and Beulah. "Marva, you are so beautiful!" Beulah exclaimed, embracing her friend.

As Monte stepped forward to greet his bride, Papa removed her hand from his arm and placed it within Monte's grasp.

"She is yours now, son." His voice cracked, and he tried to cover it with a *harrumph*.

Marva listened closely as Monte repeated his vows to her, hoping she would always remember his tender tone as he promised to love, honor, and cherish her as his own flesh. His brown eyes glistened with unshed tears as he placed the ring on her finger.

To her surprise, her own voice sounded clear and steady as she pledged to love and obey this wonderful man for as long as they both should live. After the judge pronounced them husband and wife, Myles clapped his brother on the back. Marva found herself lost in a flurry of hugs and congratulations.

More friends attended the wedding dinner, held at Boz and Amelia Martin's boardinghouse. Marva chatted with friends of all ages, seeing their faces through a happy blur. Monte remained close beside her, yet the two of them could seldom exchange a word. Once, while Myles proposed a toast and the attention of others was distracted, Monte caught his wife's hand and lifted it to his lips. Marva returned his smile and felt an immediate renewal of her spirit.

When the celebration ended and the guests finally departed, Marva followed her husband upstairs. But instead of entering their room, he continued on to the back steps. "Where are we going?" she asked in surprise.

He put his finger to his lips. "To the stables. We're driving to the next town to stay the night, then taking a train north in the morning. Don't worry; I worked it all out with your father."

Understanding dawned. "To avoid a shivaree?"

He nodded. "I have no desire to be kidnapped or paraded through town in my nightshirt."

"But would they really do that to you? You're practically a stranger in town."

"I'm taking no chances. Rumors have reached my ears, and your father suggested this plan. Watch your step and hang onto my arm while we cross the yard. It started snowing while we ate."

Monte located their bags in the loft of the Martins' stables and loaded them into a buggy. The horse waited, already harnessed, where Marva's father had left it. "What if they come searching for us?" she asked.

He helped her into the buggy and covered her with rugs. "We run that risk, but at least this way we have a chance." He climbed to his seat and clucked to the horse. "Let's just hope nobody sees us leaving town. Myles promised to provide a distraction. I think he's playing the piano and singing."

"I'm sorry to miss that, but I'd be sorrier to get shivareed." Snowflakes swirled around the side lamps like tiny moths. Marva buried her face in Monte's shoulder, yet she could hear the horse's hooves thudding in mud and spattering in puddles.

Once they were safely out of town and on the road to Bolger, she felt her husband relax. Marva sat upright. "I used to think a shivaree was funny, but now that I'm the bride, I don't care for the idea one bit." Snowflakes found their way beneath the buggy top to chill her cheeks.

"It's a crude and disrespectful custom, in my opinion," Monte said. "We can't drive faster than a walk because of ice, but I'm hoping the cold will discourage anyone from trying to follow."

"Maybe someday we'll travel to Niagara Falls, but Minocqua will be honeymoon paradise enough for me." Marva spoke with certainty.

Monte chuckled. "Don't expect it to look like it did last summer, sweetheart. We've had little snow here as yet, but I imagine we'll find plenty of it farther north."

"I don't mind. Being snowed in with you will be exciting." She hugged his arm, and he reached over to pat her mittened hands.

"Thank you." His voice held a wealth of love.

epilogue

"Did you hear that?" Marva sat bolt upright, lowering her book.

Monte loaded another log on the fire, set the screen back in place, and straightened. "No, I was making too much noise. What did you hear?"

"I think I heard a loon." Marva dumped Patches the cat from her lap, rushed to the cabin door, and stepped out on the porch. Ice still clung to the far shore, but the lodge side of the lake was open. Moonlight sparkled on its surface. How delightful was the splash of water on the shore after months of frozen silence!

Monte followed her outside. Ralph pattered down the steps and rushed toward the lake. A flock of ducks took off with a clamor of quacking and flapping wings.

"It's early yet, but you might have heard one. The lake ice is slow to break up this year." Monte wrapped his arm around his wife's waist, rested his other hand on the rail, and listened with her.

Marva shivered and hugged herself, leaning into his solid warmth. "Maybe I imagined it."

"I don't think so. Let's wait a minute more and see if it will call again. It might have been flying overhead when it called, you know." He let go of the rail and held her with both arms.

Marva could not imagine greater happiness than she had known since her marriage to Monte. The two of them clashed at times, yet they resolved their differences without acrimony;

their brief periods of discord seemed only to emphasize the general felicity of the match. Monte wrote during the day while Marva was busy with chores and projects. Every evening they spent together, reading beside the fire or simply talking. Often they planned travel vacations, perhaps to Florida or even to Europe, yet neither cared if anything actually came of their plans. For now, it was enough to be together.

Marva's parents had chosen to live inside the main lodge, where they seldom needed to step outside during winter months. Papa, however, engaged in ice fishing whenever his rheumatism would allow it. Mother kept busy sewing for the needy in the community and organizing a Concerned Women of Minocqua club.

Myles and Beulah, who was expecting again, planned to travel north and visit for an entire month during the summer, and Beulah's parents also planned to holiday at the lodge that year with their children.

Ralph trotted back to the cabin, a dark shadow with a wagging tail. Panting, he collapsed on the porch with a rattle of his bony legs against the floorboards.

Marva smiled at the familiar sound. Her two cats despised the good-natured but clumsy dog. Tigress had moved into the lodge with Marva's parents. There she earned her keep by cleaning out an invasion of deer mice. But to Marva's relief, Patches had seemed to declare and maintain an armed truce with Ralph throughout the winter. Now that the hound could spend more of his time outside, the calico cat would undoubtedly be happier in the cabin. Marva's pets could never again roam outside, since too many Northwoods beasts and birds viewed a cat as a tasty snack.

A piercing, warbling cry drifted across the waters, repeating again and again as if two birds called to each other. Monte and Marva remained quiet until the echoes died away. "A mating pair, do you think?" she asked.

"Most likely the same pair that raised two chicks down that way last summer." He pointed to his right across the lake.

"Now I can believe that spring is here," Marva said, nestling close to his chest. "Now that the loons are back."

He quoted softly, " 'For, lo, the winter is past, the rain is over and gone; the flowers appear on the earth; the time of the singing of birds is come, and the voice of the turtle is heard in our land.' "

He paused. "That works if you substitute *snow* for *rain* and *loons* for *turtles*."

"It means turtledoves."

"I always thought it meant snapping turtles."

Marva laughed and tried to push away. "I was savoring your sweet quote, and then you go and spoil it with snapping turtles. Have you no romance in your soul?"

"I have," he protested, drawing her back. "As you know very well, woman."

Again the loon's call echoed across the lake.

A Letter To Our Readers

Dear Reader:
In order that we might better contribute to your reading enjoyment, we would appreciate your taking a few minutes to respond to the following questions. We welcome your comments and read each form and letter we receive. When completed, please return to the following:

Fiction Editor
Heartsong Presents
PO Box 719
Uhrichsville, Ohio 44683

1. Did you enjoy reading *Lonely in Longtree* by Jill Stengl?
   ❑ Very much! I would like to see more books by this author!
   ❑ Moderately. I would have enjoyed it more if

   ____

   ____

   ____

2. Are you a member of **Heartsong Presents**? ❑ Yes ❑ No
   If no, where did you purchase this book? ________________

   ____

3. How would you rate, on a scale from 1 (poor) to 5 (superior), the cover dcsign? ______________________________

4. On a scale from 1 (poor) to 10 (superior), please rate the following elements.

   ____ Heroine
   ____ Hero
   ____ Setting
   ____ Plot
   ____ Inspirational theme
   ____ Secondary characters

5. These characters were special because? ______________________

____

____

6. How has this book inspired your life? ______________________

____

____

7. What settings would you like to see covered in future **Heartsong Presents** books? ______________________

____

____

8. What are some inspirational themes you would like to see treated in future books? ______________________

____

____

9. Would you be interested in reading other **Heartsong Presents** titles? ❑ Yes ❑ No

10. Please check your age range:

❑ Under 18	❑ 18-24
❑ 25-34	❑ 35-45
❑ 46-55	❑ Over 55

Name ______________________________________

Occupation ______________________________________

Address ______________________________________

City, State, Zip ______________________________________

Heartsong

HISTORICAL ROMANCE IS CHEAPER BY THE DOZEN!

Buy any assortment of twelve *Heartsong Presents* titles and save 25% off of the already discounted price of $2.97 each!

*plus $2.00 shipping and handling per order and sales tax where applicable.

HEARTSONG PRESENTS TITLES AVAILABLE NOW:

__HP463 *Crane's Bride,* L. Ford
__HP464 *The Train Stops Here,* G. Sattler
__HP467 *Hidden Treasures,* J. Odell
__HP468 *Tarah's Lessons,* T. V. Bateman
__HP471 *One Man's Honor,* L. A. Coleman
__HP472 *The Sheriff and the Outlaw,* K. Comeaux
__HP476 *Hold on My Heart,* J. A. Grote
__HP479 *Cross My Heart,* C. Cox
__HP480 *Sonoran Star,* N. J. Farrier
__HP483 *Forever Is Not Long Enough,* B. Youree
__HP484 *The Heart Knows,* E. Bonner
__HP488 *Sonoran Sweetheart,* N. J. Farrier
__HP491 *An Unexpected Surprise,* R. Dow
__HP495 *With Healing in His Wings,* S. Krueger
__HP496 *Meet Me with a Promise,* J. A. Grote
__HP500 *Great Southland Gold,* M. Hawkins
__HP503 *Sonoran Secret,* N. J. Farrier
__HP507 *Trunk of Surprises,* D. Hunt
__HP511 *To Walk in Sunshine,* S. Laity
__HP512 *Precious Burdens,* C. M. Hake
__HP515 *Love Almost Lost,* I. B. Brand
__HP519 *Red River Bride,* C. Coble
__HP520 *The Flame Within,* P. Griffin
__HP523 *Raining Fire,* L. A. Coleman
__HP524 *Laney's Kiss,* T. V. Bateman
__HP531 *Lizzie,* L. Ford
__HP535 *Viking Honor,* D. Mindrup
__HP536 *Emily's Place,* T. V. Bateman
__HP539 *Two Hearts Wait,* F. Chrisman
__HP540 *Double Exposure,* S. Laity
__HP543 *Cora,* M. Colvin
__HP544 *A Light Among Shadows,* T. H. Murray
__HP547 *Maryelle,* L. Ford
__HP551 *Healing Heart,* R. Druten
__HP552 *The Vicar's Daughter,* K. Comeaux
__HP555 *But For Grace,* T. V. Bateman
__HP556 *Red Hills Stranger,* M. G. Chapman
__HP559 *Banjo's New Song,* R. Dow
__HP560 *Heart Appearances,* P. Griffin
__HP563 *Redeemed Hearts,* C. M. Hake
__HP567 *Summer Dream,* M. H. Flinkman
__HP568 *Loveswept,* T. H. Murray
__HP571 *Bayou Fever,* K. Y'Barbo
__HP575 *Kelly's Chance,* W. E. Brunstetter
__HP576 *Letters from the Enemy,* S. M. Warren
__HP579 *Grace,* L. Ford
__HP580 *Land of Promise,* C. Cox
__HP583 *Ramshackle Rose,* C. M. Hake
__HP584 *His Brother's Castoff,* L. N. Dooley
__HP587 *Lilly's Dream,* P. Darty
__HP588 *Torey's Prayer,* T. V. Bateman
__HP591 *Eliza,* M. Colvin
__HP592 *Refining Fire,* C. Cox
__HP599 *Double Deception,* L. Nelson Dooley
__HP600 *The Restoration,* C. M. Hake
__HP603 *A Whale of a Marriage,* D. Hunt
__HP604 *Irene,* L. Ford
__HP607 *Protecting Amy,* S. P. Davis
__HP608 *The Engagement,* K. Comeaux
__HP611 *Faithful Traitor,* J. Stengl
__HP612 *Michaela's Choice,* L. Harris
__HP615 *Gerda's Lawman,* L. N. Dooley
__HP616 *The Lady and the Cad,* T. H. Murray
__HP619 *Everlasting Hope,* T. V. Bateman
__HP620 *Basket of Secrets,* D. Hunt
__HP623 *A Place Called Home,* J. L. Barton
__HP624 *One Chance in a Million,* C. M. Hake
__HP627 *He Loves Me, He Loves Me Not,* R. Druten

(If ordering from this page, please remember to include it with the order form.)